MY Especially WEIRD week with TESS

ANNA WOLTZ

TRANSLATED BY DAVID COLMER

ILLUSTRATED BY DAVID DEAN

ROCK THE BOAT

A Rock the Boat Book

First published in Great Britain, the Republic of Ireland and Australia
by Rock the Boat, an imprint of Oneworld Publications, 2023

Originally published in Dutch as *Mijn bijzonder rare week met Tess*
by Em. Querido's Uitgeverij, Amsterdam, 2013

ISBN 978-0-86154-296-3
eISBN 978-0-86154-297-0

The publisher gratefully acknowledges the support of the Dutch Foundation for Literature.

N ederlands
letterenfonds
dutch foundation
for literature

Typeset by Geethik Technologies
Printed and bound in Great Britain by Clays Ltd, Elcograf S.p.A.

This is a work of fiction. Names, characters, places and incidents are either the product
of the author's imagination or are used fictitiously, and any resemblance to actual
persons, living or dead, businesses, companies, events or locales is entirely coincidental.

For Jefta, the best dog in the world, 2001–2012

TREASURE HUNT ✗

TESS'S HOLIDAY RENTAL

The DUNES

SAM'S HOLIDAY HOME

TEXEL

The VILLAGE

TESS'S HOUSE

HENDRIK'S HOUSE

DOCTOR'S SURGERY

FERRY TO DEN HELDER

1

I saw it happen.

Dad's red jumper and my striped one were the goalposts. The sun was shining on my arms and the stiff sea breeze had decided to join the game. I chased the ball until I couldn't take another step, then stood there panting.

I could see Jasper in the distance. He wasn't doing anything. Just walking along the empty beach, staring up at the sky. Studying the white clouds drifting over the island as if he was forty, not twelve.

"Come on, Sam," Dad called. "We're in the middle of a match!"

"I know," I called back.

But I didn't move. I could feel the dry sand working its way up between my toes. I was an upside-down hourglass. I only needed to wiggle my toes and I'd gain another couple of minutes.

"Sam!" Dad shouted again.

I looked over at Jasper one last time and that was when it happened. He took another step, but instead of sand his foot landed on air. Arms flapping, he toppled into an enormous hole.

It was brilliant.

For a moment at least. Until my brother started screaming and the grin that had crept across my face vanished.

The wind whooshed and the waves roared, but nothing could drown out Jasper's screams. My blood turned cold. He didn't sound human, more like an animal.

Dad and I started running at the same time. We dashed across the loose sand as fast as we could.

We couldn't even see Jasper any more. The beach had swallowed him up.

"Jass!" I called.

"We're coming!" Dad shouted.

And then we were standing at the edge of the hole. My brother was lying at the bottom, holding his leg. His face was scrunched up and his hair was covering his eyes. Everything about him that had been so annoying these last few weeks was gone.

When he saw us, he stopped screaming. He looked up at Dad and tried to catch his breath. "I heard a snap," he said. "When I landed. There was a snap."

I shivered. It was still April. Way too cold to be standing on a windy beach with bare arms.

Dad lowered himself into the hole. When he stood in it, the sand came up to his waist. I'd only seen a hole in the ground this deep once before. That was three weeks ago, so I remembered it exactly. My whole class got to throw white rose petals into it. By the handful. I was scared the petals would run out before it was my turn, but they had an extra basket ready. I was the first one to take them out of the new basket.

Dad knelt down next to Jasper and lifted up his trouser leg.

"Careful!" I cried.

My brother didn't say anything.

"You're hurting him!"

I was scared to go too close to the edge of the hole in case the side collapsed.

Dad untied Jasper's shoelace, and I saw my brother flinch. But he still didn't make a sound.

"Give me your phone," I shouted down to Dad. "I'll call an ambulance. They can send one to the beach."

"Don't be silly," my father said.

"But he's in pain! Can't you see that? He's not saying anything, but he needs to go to hospital."

Dad nodded. "We'll take him to a doctor."

"But he can't walk."

"I'll carry him across the beach," Dad said. "Then we'll drive to the village."

"You're mad! You'll stumble while you're carrying him. Then his bones will move and grow crooked and he'll never walk again. Or he'll have a limp and then he'll never—"

"Shut up, will you?" Jasper blurted. He swiped his hair out of his eyes and looked straight at me. Now he was being Jasper again. The annoying Jasper from the last few weeks. "It hurts enough without having to listen to a little kid screeching too."

I took a step back.

Silently I watched Dad grab him under the arms and hoist him up. Jasper's face was pale and I could see him clenching his teeth. But he didn't say anything, and I knew I had to keep quiet now too.

I wasn't allowed to scream for him. I wasn't allowed to call an ambulance. He was one and a half years older than me, and by the time I was born it was already too late. He had a massive head start, but nobody said, stop, everyone back to the starting line, let's try again.

I bent down, picked a few white shells out of the sand, and tossed them one after the other into the hole. The last one landed on Jasper's head.

2

I raced back to get our jumpers while Dad pulled Jasper out of the hole. He lifted him on to his back and staggered across the beach with him. Every step, my father panted and my brother groaned. Together they sounded like a geriatric dinosaur.

I got to sit in the front of the car because Jasper needed the whole back seat to himself. We'd only arrived the night before and we didn't really know where we were. Our dark green holiday home was tucked away in the dunes. But the doctor's was in the village, so we sped past shops crammed with brightly coloured beach buckets and inflatable dolphins. Past crowded outdoor cafes and dripping ice-cream carts and fluttering flags.

Sometimes I turned back to my brother, looked at his leg and tried to imagine what it felt like. On the inside. Where it was all muscles and pulsing blood.

"What do you think?" I asked. "Does it hurt worse than anything you've ever felt before?"

"Just cos you're always thinking," Jasper said, "it doesn't mean we all do."

Right at the end of the village we found a doctor's. The low grey building didn't look like holidays at all. Dad left us in the car and ran in. I looked at my watch. Three minutes and fifteen seconds later he came back with a wheelchair.

"Phew!" he said, out of breath. "That receptionist is scary. She almost bit my nose off when she found out we hadn't called first to make an appointment. Now we have to wait until the doctor can fit us in."

"But Jasper's in pain!"

Dad shrugged. "That woman's used to people in pain. If you're not about to die, you have to make an appointment." He helped Jasper out of the car and into the wheelchair.

"Can I push?" I asked.

My father hesitated.

"I'll be careful," I said. "I promise. I know it's not a shopping trolley."

Jasper sniggered. Not too loudly, of course, because he was in pain.

"Hm," Dad said. He looked at my brother and then at me. "Fortunately I've never known you two to misbehave with shopping trolleys." He took a step to one side. "As long as you don't go too fast."

It wasn't easy to keep the wheelchair straight, but I hardly bumped into anything. The strict receptionist didn't seem to approve of me pushing it at all. She had short blonde hair and bright red lips and she waved her hand like a traffic officer. "That way! Watch out for the skirting boards, they've just been painted."

The large waiting room was full of people who looked perfectly healthy. They were wearing shorts and flip-flops with flowers on them. I parked Jasper next to a table with Lego and sat on the bench with Dad. The wall in front of us was decorated with photos of seven different kinds of beach grass. The room smelled like plasters.

I tried to sneak glances at the other people to figure out what was wrong with them. Why were they at the doctor's on such a sunny day? I couldn't tell anything from their appearance. But they were still here.

It made me think of Bella's father. Even though I didn't want to. When he had come to help with the school sports day in autumn, nobody had noticed anything. Even though he was already sick.

I fidgeted on the seat and waited. And waited some more.

"Dad?" I whispered at last. "Do you think the last dinosaur knew it was the last?"

"How do you mean?" he asked softly.

"When the last dinosaur died," I said, "did it know it was becoming extinct? That there'd never be another dinosaur again?"

Jasper looked at the beach grass as if he had nothing to do with us.

"I hope so," I said. "If it knew it was the last one, it wouldn't have felt as bad about dying. It would have been lonely otherwise."

Dad nodded. "Yes, I think so too."

Maybe he'd heard what I said. Maybe not. Answering without thinking was one of his specialities. He was a nice robot father.

"Jass?" I asked. "Do you think a dinosaur could be friends with other kinds of animals? Could it talk to—"

"Stop it!"

"But I thought—"

"It really hurts. Can't you get that into your skull?" He shook his head. "It's incredible. One half of you's a professor and the other half's a five-year-old. This leg's going to ruin my whole holiday. I don't want to talk about a lonely dinosaur who goes to visit a hedgehog for afternoon tea!"

A man with a hairy jungle on his legs chuckled and I looked at the floor. The whole waiting room was listening in.

"I'll go and sit in the car," I said.

Jasper calling me a professor didn't make any sense. To become a professor you have to finish high school first and then go to university for years. I hadn't even finished primary school. I explained that to Jasper last week, but he didn't care. He kept saying it.

I stood up and Dad gave me the car keys. "Don't drive off now!" he said, trying hard to be cheerful.

I nodded and walked out into the sun.

3

Outside, it still felt like the holidays. I was in the village and surrounded by houses but there was a salty tang to the air. The sunny pavement was covered with a thin layer of sand that had fallen off flip-flops, wet towels and inflatable animals.

I put the car keys in my pocket and started walking. Of course, I wasn't silly enough to look up at the blue sky at the same time. I wasn't planning on falling into any holes.

The keys jangled in my pocket. My head was empty. Sometimes I think too much. And sometimes I don't think at all. With me it's either one or the other. I strolled through the car park next to the doctor's and stopped.

At the back of the building there was a small patio, and in the middle of that patio there was a table with a laptop, a pot plant and a desk lamp on it. The cord from the lamp snaked over the grey paving stones but didn't go anywhere. It wasn't plugged into anything.

Sitting at the table was a blonde-haired girl with a serious face. I looked away and took a step, but she'd already seen me.

"Wait," she called.

I half turned towards her.

"Do you know anything about zebrafish?" Her voice was as serious as her face.

"Not really…" I said.

"Do you play the trumpet?"

I shook my head.

"Have you ever done a woodworking course?"

I shook my head again, and she sighed.

"Then I don't need you. Off you go."

I was too stunned to move. Again I looked at the cord that didn't go anywhere and the dusty pot plant.

And then I sneaked a look at the girl while she was peering at her laptop. She was older than me. That was obvious. And she was almost definitely not a tourist. She was wearing gleaming brown boots and a brown leather jacket. Everyone else on the island was acting like it was summer already, but not her.

"Stop!" she cried, although I was still just standing there. "I need you after all. Can you dance?"

It was simple. I had to turn and walk away. But she kept talking.

"Ballroom dancing, I mean. Like people in old movies. Or at weddings. Can you?"

"No!" I snapped. Not only could I not dance, I didn't want to either, and I wanted to make sure she knew it.

The girl smiled. "Me neither." And then she stood up. "So we're going to learn how." She typed something on the laptop, clicked a couple of times, and then all of a sudden there was music. Old-fashioned music full of violins that didn't suit the half-empty car park and the strong sea breeze. "I'm Tess, by the way," the girl said. "We'll start with the Viennese waltz." She came up to me and stopped in front of me. I felt like running away, but she grabbed my hand. She was at least a head taller than me and her fingers were sticky. I could feel her breath on my forehead. "Your right hand goes on my back," she said, as if she was the boss of the whole island. "I read all about it on the internet, but I didn't have anyone to practise with." She rested her left hand on my shoulder.

"Stop it!" I shouted. I broke free and took a step back. "That's not allowed. You can't touch people you don't know."

Tess stayed where she was, so I quickly took another step back. The old-style music was still playing – swirling, turning, dignified but cheerful with it.

"I'm eleven," I said. "If you touch me again, I'm going to the police."

"You're eleven?" She sounded surprised. "I thought you were ten. Or nine." She bent her legs a little so she was more on my level. "I'm twelve, but everyone thinks I'm older." She stepped forward again. "Please?" she asked. "It's really important for me to learn to dance before tonight."

"I don't believe you."

"The rest of my life depends on it." She looked at me and didn't look away. There were golden speckles in her brown eyes. She wasn't a robot but a real person. She saw me.

"What do you think…" I began. I cleared my throat. "Did the last dinosaur mind dying?"

She thought about it. For a long time, until the music finished and all we could hear was seagulls up in the sky. "I'd always mind dying," she said at last. "The idea of everything stopping…" She bit her lip. "But if I was the very last one, it might not be as bad. Because then I'd only be lonely anyway."

She looked at me with her speckled eyes and I nodded. I took a hesitant step forward.

"Just think," she said. "If I was the last one, I wouldn't have anyone to dance with." She ran back to the laptop and tapped the touchpad. The music started playing again. It was carousel music, but different.

"I'm Sam," I said.

She took my hand. The music was making me dizzy.

"You take one step forward with your right foot," Tess said.

I did, and at the same time she took a step back with her left foot.

"Now one step to the side with your left."

Her foot moved together with mine.

"Now your right foot follows."

I did it, and her left foot did the same.

She laughed. "That's it. We're dancing!"

4

We only stopped dancing when a man came into the car park. We were both out of breath and big grins had taken over our faces. My fingers were now almost as sticky as Tess's, but that was good. If you're both sticky, it doesn't matter.

The man came closer. His hair was white and a little too long, and he was wearing slippers. He was holding a shoebox.

Both my grandfathers are only half old. They can still run and use smartphones and chew with their own teeth. But this man was old old. He looked like a grandfather from a fairy tale.

"They won't help," he said in a sad voice. He sounded ancient, but like a little boy too.

"Who won't help?" Tess asked. She pushed a wisp of blonde hair out of her eyes.

"The police, the fire brigade, the ambulance…" The man shook his head. "I phoned all of them, but they only got angry. They said I should throw Remus away. In the bin. And that made me angry."

"Remus?" I asked.

He nodded. With trembling hands, he carefully raised the lid of the shoebox. Lying on a bed of cotton wool was a stiff yellow bird. Its scrawny legs were sticking up in the air. Its eyes were shut.

I'd seen dead birds before, but never this close. And never arranged solemnly in a box. I wanted to shut my eyes, but I was still alive – I had to look.

The old man looked too. Silently he stared at the little bird, and I could see that he really loved Remus.

"Just a moment," Tess said. She pulled me away by the arm. "That's Mr Vis," she whispered. "He lives around the corner from us. Sometimes I see him shuffling round the supermarket with an almost empty shopping basket. He's been alone for way too long. He really should go to an old people's home, but he doesn't want to."

I looked at him as he stood there obediently waiting. I couldn't imagine ever getting that old. Or ever standing in a car park with a dead canary. But there was one thing I could imagine. His not wanting to put Remus in the bin. You can't just throw away an animal that has a name.

"We have to help him," I said softly.

"How?"

"We can bury Remus for him. I was at a funeral three weeks ago. I know how."

Tess tilted her head to one side. "You're here on holiday, right? And now you want to arrange a funeral for a dead canary. Don't you think that's a bit weird?"

"You dance in car parks!"

She started laughing. "Yeah…I guess I kind of like weird. The kids in my class don't. But I do."

"Me too," I replied without thinking and without knowing if it was true.

"Okay." She nodded. "We'll organise a funeral. But we have to keep it simple. I've still got loads to do."

She hurried back to the fairy-tale grandfather. "We're going to have something to eat now, but then we'll help you give Remus a funeral. What's your house number again?"

"Number seven," he said, slightly surprised.

I came up alongside Tess. "We need some information about Remus for the ceremony. What were his favourite flowers?"

He scrunched his bristly eyebrows. "Young man," he said. "This is a canary we're talking about. A very macho canary. Remus was not a flower lover."

"Oh," I said.

Tess was giggling, but I ignored her.

"What did he like?" I asked politely.

"Spinach," the old man said. "And cherries. The colour yellow. And the newspaper. I read it to him every day." He coughed, and looked unsure of himself again. "So you'll come by this afternoon? Really?"

"Really," I said.

Tess nodded. "Promise."

The old man didn't say anything else. He turned and slowly began his journey back home. You could tell from his bent back how carefully he was holding Remus.

Tess sighed, then swung her arms angrily. "Why do the last years of your life have to be so stupid?"

"Maybe…" I watched the man struggling to put one foot in front of the other. "Maybe so you get used to things being stupid. So you don't mind as much when you die."

"But I don't want to get used to it!"

"I do," I said, because suddenly I got it. You had to keep your eyes open and get used to things being stupid. That was the only way.

"Shall we do one last waltz?" Tess asked, once Mr Vis had disappeared out of sight. "I need to cheer up again."

I nodded.

She ran over to the laptop and in no time we were swirling around the sunny car park again.

One-two-three, one-two-three…

One-two-three, one—

Just then Dad called my name. We froze in the middle of a dance step.

5

Dad and Jasper were staring at us.

My brother was still in the wheelchair and Dad was standing behind it. The sun was shining on their brown hair. Their faces were pale from winter, and they were looking at me as if I'd just landed on the moon.

"I'm waltzing," I said casually – but I felt like I was floating. That was partly from dancing, but mainly because of the look in their eyes. They'd never looked at me like this before. I felt like waving a big bright flag. Here I am! I'm dancing with a girl with speckled eyes. "This is Tess," I said. "She's twelve."

Dad and Jasper were still staring. They kept it up for so long it started to get a bit uncomfortable.

"My brother fell into a hole this morning," I told Tess. "That's why we're here at the doctor's."

Now Dad could finally talk again. "The doctor thinks Jasper has broken his ankle."

"Ow," Tess said. "You'll have to take the ferry back to Den Helder."

"Why?" I asked. "Don't you have plaster here?"

She shook her head. "There's no X-ray machines on Texel. You have to go to Den Helder for that. We've got lots of sheep and tourists, but no hospital." She looked at Jasper. "Falling into that hole was not a good idea."

"No," he said. "I've worked that out by now too."

Her hand was still on my shoulder and I saw my brother looking at it. I wasn't moving, so the hand stayed where it was.

"Hey, Jasper…" Tess thought for a moment. "You haven't by any chance ever done a woodworking course, have you?"

I let out a giggle.

"Or maybe you know how to play the trumpet?"

He didn't get it. And he didn't like weird anyway. "Are we going?" he asked.

My father nodded. He started pushing the wheelchair towards the car, but I still didn't move.

Tess and I looked at each other. We had a busy day ahead. We had to organise a whole funeral and there was sure to be another dance I had to learn. I didn't have time to go anywhere.

"I'll stay here," I said.

Dad turned and looked at me in surprise. "I can't leave you here by yourself."

"Mum's here too."

"Don't be silly. You know she can't look after you today."

"But—"

"I'm really not in the mood for this, Sam. I have to take your brother to the hospital. Stop whining and come with us. Now!"

I hung my head and started to walk towards the car. Who came up with the rule that you can't leave a kid somewhere by themselves? Because of that one person, kids all over the world have missed out on at least a thousand adventures. It wasn't fair.

"Sam's father," Tess shouted. "Wait!" She ran over to Dad. "Your son can stay with me today. My mother's the receptionist here at the surgery. We're going to have something to eat and then I can show Sam the village. I know everyone here, and it's very safe. The children in my class almost never get hurt. Just Ellen last year when the roof of the pigsty gave way and she fell twelve feet... But fortunately she landed on the pigs and not the concrete floor."

Dad's mouth dropped open but no sound came out of it.

Tess looked up at him. "At the hospital you always have to wait forever. You have to sit still and whisper until it drives you nuts. Everyone knows that. Really, it's much more convenient for Sam to stay here..."

Her voice sounded as sweet as honey. And Dad wasn't used to girls who held their heads tilted to one side. He probably didn't know anyone with speckled eyes.

"I'll give you my number," Tess said. "Then you can call whenever you like."

Dad looked at me helplessly. "Do you really want to stay here?" he asked. "With this girl?"

I nodded. "I want to stay here. With this girl."

6

Secretly I was a bit surprised when Dad and Jasper really did drive off without me. Dad even stuck his hand out of the window to wave. "I'll pick you up soon as we're back!" Then they turned the corner and disappeared.

"Did you save his number?" I asked Tess.

She laughed. "Shall I call him for you? Would you like to hear his voice for a moment?"

Luckily I didn't have to answer, because the back door opened. The strict receptionist – the one with short hair and red lips – came out with a tray full of food. It was only now she was walking that I saw how tall she was. Way taller than Dad.

"Mum!" Tess cried cheerfully. She pulled me along by the arm. "This is Sam. He's having lunch with us."

She quickly closed the laptop so her mother couldn't see the screen. Then she started arranging bread and cheese and strawberries and mini Mars bars on the table.

Tess's mother stretched and yawned. That red mouth of hers really opened wide. "So you're starting on boyfriends already?" she asked her daughter, inspecting me carefully. With eyebrows raised, she studied my arms, legs and hair. "Well, I'll be," she said finally. "A tiny tourist." She sniggered. "At least he won't boss you around. That's something."

Two other women in white coats and trousers came out with chairs, and a little later the five of us were eating. I didn't say anything because I didn't know if tiny tourists were allowed to talk. And nobody missed my voice because they were all babbling away as if the world was about to end.

I chewed in silence. I was still thinking about the pigs Ellen landed on. Did they get hurt? Or were they mostly just shocked by a girl suddenly falling through the roof?

After two sandwiches and four mini Mars bars, Tess stood up. "We have to get to work." She slid her laptop into a backpack and beckoned. "Come on, Sam!"

Her mother sniggered again and waved me goodbye.

I didn't wave back.

"Was she scary?" Tess asked, when we were walking down the street a little later.

"Um…"

"Most men think she's scary."

"Maybe she could try being a bit friendlier," I said. "Most men don't like being called tiny. That's what I think."

She nodded and was quiet. "I don't think she minds," she said after a while. "That men are scared of her, I mean. Not them being smaller than her. She thinks that's stupid."

I kicked a stone. "I think she needs to get used to it."

Tess giggled.

We walked past an outdoor cafe full of fathers and mothers and children. They were wearing big sunglasses and eating pancakes for lunch because it was the holidays.

At school, I was used to always being the smallest. But now, with all these sunglasses turned towards Tess and me, it felt new. Like looking in a mirror for the first time.

"What about your father?" I asked to change the subject in my head. "Is he scared of your mother too?"

"No idea," Tess said. "I don't know him."

I stopped walking. "You don't know your father?"

She shook her head.

"How can you not know your father?"

She crossed her arms. "People are so nosy! If I say I don't know my father, they want to know right away how come. Always. Over and over again. I don't ask you how your parents made you, do I?"

I winced.

"Exactly," Tess said. She sighed. "Okay… Thirteen years ago my mother was dating my father. They went off to travel the world together, but after a few months Mum got sick of it. She came back home, and my father kept travelling. But when she was back here, Mum found out she was expecting a baby. That was me."

"What did your father say?"

"Nothing. Mum didn't tell him because they'd broken up. But she didn't mind having a kid. So she had me by herself."

Fluttering over our heads were the pennants of a fish and chip shop. It smelled like fried batter and mayonnaise.

"So your father doesn't even know you exist?"

She shook her head.

I looked at her. For twelve years this girl had been able to breathe and move and look around, but her father didn't know she was alive. Her mother had kept her a secret. Just imagine. When her father thought of all the people in the world, he didn't know one of them was his own daughter.

"Come on, tiny tourist!" Tess started walking again. "You've stared at me long enough. We have a funeral to arrange. What do we need to do?"

I bit my lip. Remus had slipped my mind completely. "Is there a supermarket here?" I asked after a while.

"We're not on the moon. We do have supermarkets."

"And a shop with tissue paper?"

She nodded. "Even that. Fathers are out of stock at the moment, but we've got everything else."

I tried not to stare at her any more, but it wasn't easy.

So her father didn't know she existed. But she knew *he* existed, somewhere in the world. He had to, otherwise she would never have been born. Or maybe he wasn't alive any more? Maybe he'd been eaten by a shark during his trip around the world. Or fallen into a volcano.

"Couldn't you google him?" I asked. "Then you could get to know him. Tell him you exist."

She shook her head and looked at two seagulls fighting over an empty chip box. "Mum won't tell me his name."

"What?"

She was still watching the grey-and-white birds. "Not till I'm eighteen. She thinks it's fine the way it is, with the two of us. We don't need a man."

"And she just decided that for you?" I asked.

"No." She stuck her nose in the air. "My mother put a lot of serious thought into it. And then she came to the conclusion that it's better like this."

"Oh," I said.

7

An hour later we rang the fairy-tale grandfather's doorbell. I was nervous because Tess had told me I was in
charge of the funeral. She'd never been to one. She
didn't know any dead people.

"You're here!" he exclaimed, as if he hadn't been
expecting us to keep our promise. Maybe he was
only used to ordinary children. Children who never
organise funerals.

Tess went in first, of course. She'd already forgotten
I was in charge.

"Hello, Mr Vis," she said. "I'm Tess, and this is
Sam."

It was dark in the hall and it smelled odd. It smelled
like Christmas, even though we'd just had Easter.

"Call me Hendrik," the man said. "Not Mr Vis.
That only makes me feel old."

He shuffled ahead into the living room. The
furniture was brown and dusty, like I'd imagined.

But the walls were different. They were covered from floor to ceiling with newspaper clippings. Not boring photos of swaying beach grass, but photos you couldn't help but look at. A big one of galloping horses with billowing manes and tails. A funny one of a tortoise on scales. And a fabulous one of a gorilla gazing lovingly at a rabbit. Next to the photo it said SAMANTHA HAS A PET BUNNY.

I walked straight up to the wall and read about Samantha the gorilla, who lived in an American zoo. After her male partner died, she got lonely, so the zookeepers gave her a rabbit as a pet. To be on the safe side, they made a hatch first so the rabbit could escape. But it didn't want to escape. It wanted to stay with Samantha.

"Now she shares her food with a rabbit," I heard Hendrik say softly. "Fabulous. That's why I'm still alive. To read about a gorilla who's in love with a rabbit."

I turned around. The old man was standing by the window next to an empty birdcage. On the table I could see Remus's shoebox and a large plate with slices of sponge cake on it.

"I bought that for you two," Hendrik said. "That's what you do after a funeral, isn't it? Eat cake?"

I nodded.

"Tess told me you have a garden," I said. "Shall we go outside? Then we can choose a spot for Remus."

It seemed to take a long time before the hole was deep enough. We only had one small spade, so Tess used a soup spoon. Hendrik had shown us where to dig: next to the apple tree. Above us the blossoms were swaying gently. The buds were pink, the flowers white as snow.

I looked up at the flower-filled branches and the blue sky overhead and thought: on a day like this you should be burying a prince. Glorious sunshine, a blossoming apple tree – and all for a bird? Nothing but feathers and tiny little bones…

But that tree wasn't blossoming for us. The sun wasn't shining for Remus.

Finally, the grave was dug. We looked at the little canary one last time, then wrapped the shoebox in yellow tissue paper. Remus's favourite colour. While Tess picked up her laptop, I put the shoebox in the hole. Together we looked down at the yellow box in the dirt.

"Would you like to say something?" I asked Hendrik.

He nodded. He straightened his back as best he could and folded his hands together. "Remus," he said in a solemn voice. "In my life I've had dogs and cats and rabbits. And I had you. I loved all of you and I shared my food with you." He coughed. "My living room's quiet without you. And yet I'm glad you died before me. What would you have done without me?" He cleared his throat. "I'm too old now for something new, so you were my last pet. I'll miss you. Goodbye, Remus." He took a step back.

Everything was quiet for a moment, and then Tess tapped her laptop.

Again there was music under the sunny sky. This time it wasn't dance music, but a song, "Wind Beneath my Wings". Tess and I had chosen it together.

While the singer sang about flying higher than an eagle, I reached for the bag from the supermarket. We let light green spinach leaves float down on to Remus's box and dropped some shiny cherries next to it. The apple tree shed a sprinkling of blossoms over us.

With the music playing quietly in the background, Tess and I knelt next to the hole. First I threw a handful of earth on to the shoebox, then it was Tess's turn. I looked at her and saw that her lip was quivering.

We hadn't known Remus, and he was only a canary. But he was dead, and that made me think of all the other animals and people who were dead, and all the animals and people who were still going to die.

And suddenly I understood. I was thinking of everyone in the whole world.

Including Dad.

And Mum.

And me too.

8

We walked around the corner, our stomachs full of cake. We were on Tess's street now, but I couldn't stop thinking about Hendrik. I'd never experienced anything like it before. A grown-up saying "thank you" to me at least seventeen times!

And every time Hendrik said "thank you", Tess and I would take another bite of cake. It was the only thing left we could still do for him. Eat his cake.

"I always thought it was weird," Tess said, running her hand over a bristly hedge, "when people said a funeral was beautiful. But now I understand."

"You almost cried!"

"That was…" She hesitated. "It was good crying. Like when a film's sad."

"Do you cry at films?" I asked in surprise. "With tears? And a runny nose?"

"You're a boy," Tess said. "You don't get it. Boys don't have any feelings."

I didn't answer. I was thinking of Bella's father again. When Bella read her poem at his funeral three weeks ago, the whole class cried. Including the boys. And our teacher, Mr Welling. And Bella's grandfather.

Tess had opened the gate to a front garden full of daisies and was halfway to the blue front door when her phone rang.

"Is it my dad?" I asked, but she gestured for me to keep quiet.

She stood up straight and twisted her mouth into a peculiar smile before answering. "Texel Gold Holiday Homes!" She sounded like she'd landed a role in a toothpaste ad. "Hello, Mr Faber, how good of you to call…" She listened and I saw her cheeks turning red. "You're already on the ferry?" She was swinging one restless foot through the daisies. "Of course, Mr Faber. One hour from now. I'll make sure someone is at the house to give you the key. Bye!" She put the phone back in her pocket and looked at me. She was out of breath even though she was standing completely still. "I have to go," she said nervously. "We have a house in the dunes we rent out sometimes. I have to go and give them the key. I thought he was arriving this evening, but he's almost here already."

"I don't mind coming with you," I said.

"No," she snapped. "You can't come. He…" She bit her lip and turned back to the front door. "I have to feed Mog," she mumbled. "Buy flowers, open the windows, put out the programme…"

Sometimes being this small is useful. I walked in behind Tess and she hardly noticed. Her house wasn't big, but there was loads to see. All the colours were glaring, the wallpaper had gigantic flowers on it and there were five enormous cactuses on the windowsill. It looked like the kind of place a tall woman who men were scared of would feel right at home.

Tess hurried through to the kitchen and quickly spooned cat food into a garish pink bowl. A fat cat purred past her legs. Tess stroked the cat's round belly and whispered something to her.

Then she stood up and looked me in the eye.

"I only know three aquarium fish off by heart! I've only just learned how to waltz and I don't know a thing about jazz…" She shook her head. "I can't do it. I'm never too scared to do anything, but now I am. I'm too scared!"

I had no idea what she was talking about. I only knew one thing for certain: I didn't want her to leave me here by myself.

Sometimes being left behind is great. With parents out of the way, you can have adventures. But I didn't want to be all by myself now. Not right after burying someone. Not in a house full of cactuses.

"I'll come with you," I said, trying to sound grown-up. As if I was helping her, instead of trying to arrange things to suit myself. "You have to buy flowers first, right?"

She nodded.

"Have you got the keys to the holiday home?"

She nodded again. But then she shook her head. "You haven't even got a bike! And Mum'll be home soon. She's not allowed to find out I'm gone."

It was making less and less sense. If Tess and her mother rented out a holiday home, surely they were used to tourists needing the key? What difference did it make if her mother found out Mr Faber was arriving a little early?

"You can give me a backie," I said in a calm, grown-up voice. "And you can call your mother and tell her you're having dinner with us tonight. Then we'll have plenty of time."

She hesitated. Her cheeks were blazing red. Her hands kept fidgeting.

"Fine," she said at last. "But you're not allowed to say anything!" She grabbed me by the arm. "When we're at the house, later, you don't say a single word. Promise?"

I could feel her fingers through my jumper. They were digging into my arm, as if she was never going to let go.

"I won't say anything," I said. "I promise."

She nodded. "Okay. Then we have to hurry. Come on!"

9

The wind blew through my hair and the world flew past. I could feel Tess's stomach muscles contracting as she pedalled as hard as she could. I'd wrapped one arm around her waist to keep myself from falling off the back. In my free hand, I was holding a bunch of yellow tulips.

We were riding through the dunes on a wide cycle path without bumps or potholes. We rode up the hills slowly, then zoomed downhill faster than the speed of light. Growing along the path were elderly pines with bent trunks, and oaks that were bursting with new green leaves.

This was my first time on the island of Texel and I already loved it. In the village the crowded cafes full of tourists might drive you crazy, but out here I couldn't see anyone. Only Tess, who was pedalling and panting and alive.

For a moment I thought about my brother. Poor Jasper. With a broken ankle he wouldn't be able to ride a bike all week. But then I remembered how annoying he'd been acting. I didn't have a nice brother any more, I had one who could only talk about the school musical. One who fell in a hole because he refused to play football with Dad and me.

"Made it!" Tess gasped.

Without slowing down, she swerved into the drive of a small brown house. It had a flat roof and floral curtains. Tess ran up the wooden steps, opened the door and raced through the house like a whirlwind: windows open, tulips in a vase, brochures and information on the table – and then she was standing next to me again on the veranda.

Her forehead was damp with sweat. Her feet kept moving even though she was standing still. I'd only known her for half a day, but I knew this wasn't normal. Maybe for other girls, but not for Tess.

"I think I'm going to faint," she said, and suddenly she really did look pale, "I'm not joking, I'm about to faint."

"Come on," I said. "This Mr Faber guy's not that scary, is he?"

"You have no idea."

"I thought you rented it out all the time?"

"But this is my father!"

She'd shouted it and immediately clapped a hand over her mouth.

We heard a car in the distance.

"Here he comes," she whispered.

"Your father? But you said you didn't know him."

She shook her head.

"I don't. I mean, I've never met him. But a few months ago I found out his name." She grabbed me by the shoulders. "You keep your mouth shut, okay! He doesn't know a thing. He doesn't know who I am – he doesn't even know I exist. And maybe it should stay that way. I—"

A blue Saab was coming up the drive and Tess let go of me. She wiped her forehead and I saw that her hand was shaking. For a moment I thought I could hear her heart, but it was mine.

The car pulled up next to the house. The heavy engine stopped rumbling and all at once it was strangely quiet. I didn't even dare blink. I didn't want to miss a second.

Finally the car door opened and a tall man got out. He ran his fingers through his hair and turned his head to check out the surroundings. He looked younger than Dad, but that might have been because of his clothes. He was wearing tattered jeans and a T-shirt with a smiley face on it.

And then the passenger door swung open too. A woman with red hair got out and I held my breath. Who was this? Had Tess known a woman was coming too? I shot a glance at her face but couldn't see anything. No surprise. No recognition.

The tall man came up to the veranda. He held out a hand to shake Tess's, and then mine.

"Hugo Faber," he said in a friendly voice.

He looked at me and in a flash, I noticed. He had speckled eyes.

Otherwise he didn't look like Tess at all. His hair was darker, his face was more angular. But with those brown eyes I knew instantly: this was her father. It was true. He was on the planet. He existed. And now he was here.

"Hi!" said the red-headed woman. "I'm Elise."

"Hello," I mumbled, shaking her hand too.

Tess didn't say a thing. She just stood there staring at Hugo Faber.

I clenched my fists and tried to understand what was going on inside her head. What if I'd never seen Dad before? If I didn't have the slightest idea what kind of things he said. How he moved and laughed and looked angry. What would it be like to then see him for the first time in my life? How would it feel?

Would I be mad with joy? Or would I think, I don't know him. We've never been to the park together. He doesn't know what kind of cake I had on my fifth birthday. He wasn't there the first time I went on a plane.

Tess stayed silent. Her face was still frozen.

Elise tried another smile and Hugo's eyes went from Tess to me and back again. The silence was getting heavier by the second.

So I said, "Welcome to Texel."

I'd promised not to say anything. But this was an emergency. I couldn't let Tess's father start off thinking she was a nutcase right away.

"Did you find it all right?" I asked. My voice sounded almost normal.

I didn't hear what Hugo Faber and Elise said in reply. I watched their mouths moving, but their words didn't get through to my brain. I moved a bit closer to Tess and grabbed her hand. I squeezed it. Gently first, then harder. And then even harder.

"Oh!" she said, cutting Elise off mid-sentence. "I'll just explain how the TV and the microwave work. And your programme is ready too. Come in."

She led us into the living room. The curtains were moving softly in the wind. The yellow tulips were on the table.

"We keep the remote control here," Tess said. "You press this button first, and then you can change channels like this…"

Hugo nodded.

"And the heating?" he asked. "It can get pretty cold at night this time of year."

"Of course," Tess said, walking into the hall with her father tagging along behind her.

He followed her without knowing she was his daughter.

10

The tour was over way too fast. Hugo and Elise thanked us and went back to the car for their bags.

Tess and I walked over to the bike. Hugo gave us a cheery wave, then disappeared into the house.

"What do you think?" I whispered. Now we were out of sight, I wanted to jump and yell. I was about to explode with curiosity. How had Tess found out who her father was? And what was he doing here?

She grabbed her bike without a word. I had barely enough time to jump on the back before she tore off.

"Did you see his eyes?" I shouted over the wind. "They had speckles, like yours! And he's even taller than your mother." I laughed. "I bet he wasn't scared of her."

The warm smell of pine trees filled my nose with every breath. The oaks seemed even greener than before. The blood was rushing through my veins.

"Could you tell right away he was your father? And was it weird to shake hands with him? I mean—"

The bike squealed to a halt. I jumped off in the nick of time, otherwise we would have fallen over.

Tess spun round to face me. "You stupid idiot!" she shouted. "You just don't get it."

I was too surprised to reply.

"How could I tell if he was my father or not? I don't know him, do I? I met him for the first time. I looked at him and I didn't feel a thing. Nothing at all."

I took a step back because she was spitting the words out at full volume.

"Nothing?" I asked. "Not even a quiver or a sigh or a teensy little tingle?"

Slowly, with her eyes turned down, she shook her head.

I looked at her and felt all kinds of things at once.

"Now I know," she said in a hoarse voice. "Grown-ups are just fooling us. They act like family's something special." She swallowed. "But it's really nothing at all."

She wiped a wisp of hair out of her face.

"Do you know that show on TV? Where adopted people who are forty or something go in search of their parents? Their birth parents. Then they all give each other big, weepy hugs somewhere in China or Bolivia."

I nodded. It was a show Mum watched.

"I always thought it's so beautiful," Tess said. "They can tell. They can feel that that wrinkly old man is their father. But it's not true! They're acting. Pretending. Because you don't feel anything…"

In the distance a family with four children were approaching. Six merry voices singing about rowing boats while riding bikes.

I looked at them and clenched my fists. I didn't want it to be nonsense. I didn't want grown-ups to pretend.

"Hugo Faber is not my father," Tess said, after the family had disappeared over the next hill. "He's just a man in worn-out jeans and a childish T-shirt." She sniffed. "Just a man who happened to sleep with my mother."

"Yuck," I said. And then, "That's not true."

She acted like family didn't mean anything. But why did Mum and Dad take time off to come to Texel with us? Why did me and Jasper make breakfast in bed for Mum on Mother's Day? And why did Bella cry her heart out when her father died? What was the point of all that, if it was fake?

"You have to get to know him," I said. "When he knows who you are, he'll act different."

"I don't want him any more." She shook her head. "The father I made up was way more fun."

"You're mad," I said. "What would you rather have, a made-up father or a real one?"

"That man is not my father."

"Think about it!" I shouted impatiently. "Half of you comes from your mother. The other half comes from Hugo Faber. He's your father. It's that simple."

She looked at me. "You call that simple?"

"Yeah. I do."

"Wow." She put one foot on the pedal. "You think you're smart. You think you understand everything. But you don't get it at all." She gave me a little wave. "Bye, Sam."

And off she rode.

It took me thirteen seconds to get my voice back.

"Wait," I called out. Then I started running. "You can't leave me behind!"

But that was exactly what she did.

She rode off without looking back. Her blonde hair fluttering in the wind. The low sun shining on her bike. I ran as fast as I could, but it was impossible to catch up.

On top of the next dune I stopped to catch my breath. Tess was still pedalling hard. As I watched, she got smaller and smaller. And then she was gone.

11

Tess didn't come back. That's what I was expecting – for her to come back.

That's what Jasper would do. He might ride off for a while, but no matter how angry he was, he'd always come back. I knew that for sure.

But not Tess. I knew that now too.

I walked up to a pine tree next to the path and started kicking the trunk. "You're the stupid idiot!" I yelled. As loud as I could, to give the seagulls earache. "You don't get it! You're the dumb one!"

Bits of bark flew through the air and pain pierced my toes. I kicked again and again – and then it was over.

I stood there panting. I looked around, but the cycle path was empty. So was the sky. And the grass. I'd chased everyone away.

My toes were burning and my heart was thumping. I couldn't believe it. Tess knew I didn't have a phone.

She knew I didn't know my way around. But she'd still left me.

All the singing families were home having dinner, so there was nobody to give me a lift. I bit my lip. There was no other choice: I had to walk.

So that's what I did. I started walking. I knew which direction, but otherwise I didn't have a clue. I may even have cried a little. But nobody saw me, so I could pretend it wasn't happening.

Stupid Tess, I thought with every step I took.

Stupid Tess.

Stupid Tess.

Tomorrow the police would find me here. Shrivelled up from hunger and dried out from thirst. Tess would feel horribly guilty, of course. At my funeral everyone would tell her how smart I was. How well I understood things. And then she'd burst into tears.

I started to gradually walk faster because I wasn't actually that keen on shrivelling up in the dunes. My trainers were silent on the path. The low sun was shining in my eyes. I was out on a forced march while Jasper and Dad were at the hospital. While Tess sped further away on her shiny bike. While Hugo Faber unpacked his suitcase.

That guy was her father. And at the same time he wasn't. I understood that perfectly. I understood that it was weird to suddenly meet him. I understood how complicated that was.

Every time I puffed my way up to the top of a hill, I thought, now I'll see her. Now she'll be waiting for me.

But she wasn't.

I was starting to get really hungry and my mouth was dry. It wasn't only my toes that were hurting now, but the soles of my feet too, and my heels. Much longer, and my fingers would start to wither away…

And then I saw a road I recognised and stared at it as if I'd spotted a dinosaur in the wild. That narrow brick road led to our holiday home! I started running and none of the aches and pains mattered any more.

I'd never seen the house before yesterday, but I was still overjoyed to spot its green roof. The sliding glass doors to the patio were open, so I flew straight into the living room.

"Sam!" Mum was sitting on the sofa with a blanket wrapped around her shoulders. She had her legs up and a bowl of soup on her lap. My own mother. I went straight up and hugged her. I never did that usually. But now I did.

She wasn't wrinkly. She didn't live in Bolivia and I'd already known her for eleven years. Sometimes there were days when she couldn't look after me because she got migraines. They're the worst headaches in the whole world. When she had one, the slightest sound and the slightest movement made her feel sick. She couldn't eat or drink, read or go to the beach.

But now she was eating something, and that meant the migraine was over. She was back.

12

That night, Mum and I had the house to ourselves. Jasper needed an operation on his ankle and they could only do it the next day. He had to stay overnight in the hospital and Dad had booked a room in a hotel in Den Helder.

I was on the top of an unfamiliar bunk bed and it took me ages to fall asleep. First I thought about my brother, alone in one of those white beds on wheels. In pain and without his family.

And then I thought about Hugo Faber, who had a family but didn't know. Women never have a child without noticing. But men can.

I turned on to my other side.

I thought it was really mean of Tess's mother not to tell Hugo. Surely you can't keep a whole person secret?

I turned back again.

I still didn't understand how Hugo Faber had ended up here. How had Tess lured him on to the island without giving away who she was? How had she done that?

That question kept waltzing around inside my head. It made me dizzy, but it wouldn't stop dancing. It was so weird. Today I had experienced one day of someone else's life. And just like that, it was over. Tess was mad at me, and I'd never hear what happened next.

When the nightmare came, I didn't even realise I was asleep.

I was on the beach, standing at the edge of a hole. A man was lying stretched out on the bottom with his eyes shut. There were people gathered around me. Someone rested their hand on my shoulder.

"It's so terrible your father's dead," the people said. "You must be very sad."

I looked at the man in the hole. "That's not my father!" I cried.

"Of course it is," the people said, while petals rained down out of the sky. "Don't you recognise your own father?"

"It's not him!"

The petals were fluttering into my mouth and eyes. I wiped them away, but they kept coming. And then all at once, I saw. It was him. It was Dad lying there in that hole. I screamed.

13

The next day I woke up early, opened my eyes and discovered I was in the big bed next to Mum. I couldn't remember how I got there.

We toasted stale currant buns that were left over from the drive up and ate breakfast outside in the sun.

The plastic chairs were still wet with dew, and invisible birds were singing in the trees. I saw a rabbit shoot off through the grass and took a deep breath. The salty air tingled in my lungs and almost gave me goosebumps on my arms.

But I still couldn't stop thinking about the story that was continuing without me.

Tess was probably sitting at her bright green kitchen table with her mother. Eating mountains of muesli to grow extra tall and talking about pigsties and tiny tourists.

And all the while Tess's mother was completely clueless. She didn't know Hugo Faber was on the island. She didn't know Tess had met him yesterday. And she didn't know her daughter never wanted to see him again.

"Shall we walk to the village this morning?" Mum asked cheerfully. "Then we can do some shopping and rent some bikes."

"Walk?" I asked. "Is that a joke?"

"It's only half an hour. Otherwise we'll just sit around waiting for Dad and Jasper and the car."

I sighed. My feet were still mushed from yesterday and for the first time in my life I'd woken up with shin-ache. Mum didn't know that, of course. I'd told her about Tess, but not about Hugo Faber and my lonely hike. She had no idea I'd almost been eaten alive by dune bunnies.

I was going to say no, but then it occurred to me that we might run into Tess in the village. By chance, in the supermarket. Or on the street. We'd had a fight – I hadn't forgotten that – but even when you've had an argument with someone, you can still accidentally happen to walk down the same street.

"Okay," I said, and a little later we set off. Mum was wearing a blue polka-dot dress and I was in shorts. It was fun to act like it was already summer.

We walked past enormous fields full of frolicking lambs and dusty mother sheep. The big lambs were playing and grazing with the grown-up animals, but the little ones were just standing there on wobbly legs with googly eyes, as if they'd only seen the world for the first time today. And maybe they had.

"Mum?" I asked. "Who's smarter – you or Dad?"

"That's a weird question," she said. And then she laughed. "Dad's better at maths. But I don't make as many spelling mistakes. And I'm a lot better with computers. At least I don't hit them when they play up."

"But if you both had to do a test," I said, "a real test like the high school admission test, who'd get the best marks?"

She was quiet for a moment. Then she said, "You know I don't want you talking about this any more, Sam."

"But it's Jasper's test I'm not allowed to talk about! This is a completely different question."

She didn't answer, and I kicked the sand. For two months now, I hadn't been allowed to talk about Jasper's high school admissions test. Not since the day he'd got his results. The only thing my parents didn't tell me was what would happen if I did talk about it. They probably didn't know themselves. We have rules in our family, but no punishments.

Today the village was even busier. The cafes were packed and the shops were overflowing. On Texel you had the choice of three souvenirs: something shaped like a sheep, something made from a sheep, or a sheep made from a sheep. That was all.

We walked on and on and on…

"Where are we going?" I asked anxiously.

"To the bike hire place. It's at the end of this street."

"But that's where the doctor's is!" I cried. "I've already been there. I was there yesterday."

My mother looked at me with surprise. "Is that a problem?"

I wanted to explain, but I couldn't. I didn't even know where to start. So we kept walking.

I shook my head. This wasn't working out. The idea was to bump into Tess by accident. Not to walk right past her with my mother.

We came closer and closer to the doctor's surgery.

Maybe she wouldn't be there. I hoped so. At that moment I would have done pretty much anything to be able to stop walking. Even break my ankle. Though that would have been pointless. We'd have had to go to the doctor's then anyway.

Five more steps, four, three – and then we saw the patio at the back door. The table with the pot plant and the desk lamp was there again. And sitting at the table was Tess, as if nothing had happened.

She'd shouted at me and called me stupid. Then she'd left me behind in the dunes. I should have been angry at her. That was obvious.

But she had her blonde hair in a shiny ponytail that curled at the bottom. And her brown jacket still matched her eyes. I tried not to notice. I tried telling myself that I was a boy, and boys don't care if things match.

But that wasn't true. Because I was a boy. And I did care.

"Oh, what a coincidence!" Mum stopped and looked at me. "Is that the girl you told me about? The one who showed you the village? Nice, now I can meet her too. Let's say hello."

14

It was a disaster, but there was nothing I could do about it. Tess had already seen us.

"Hello!" my mother called cheerfully. She walked across the car park in her polka-dot dress and on to the patio.

Tess didn't say a word. She looked over at me.

I wanted to explain that it hadn't been my idea to come looking for her, but I couldn't. Not in front of Mum, who had already started talking to Tess.

"It's so nice to meet you," she said. "Sam told me how much fun you had together yesterday."

Tess raised her eyebrows and I felt like shrivelling up. Once, in Reception, I wet my pants at school. Actually, I wet my yellow chick costume because that day I was acting in a play as Hatched Easter Egg Number Five. But that was nothing compared to today. It couldn't get worse than this.

But it did!

The back door opened and Tess's mother came out. This time her lips were bright pink and she looked even taller than yesterday. "Little Sam!" she cried. "My favourite tiny tourist..." She looked at my mother. "You must be Sam's mother." She shook Mum's hand. "So these two are thick as thieves!"

Slowly Tess's cheeks started burning as much as mine. I saw her looking round, but she was as trapped as I was.

Her mother laughed. "First thing this morning, Tess was busy packing a picnic basket. Nice that you two are going off together again."

"Mum!" Tess was furious.

Her mother clapped a hand over her mouth. "Oh! Was it supposed to be a surprise?" She shook her head. "I'm sorry, sweetheart – I didn't realise Sam didn't know."

"A picnic," Mum said. "Lovely!"

I looked at Tess. Yesterday she'd left me behind in the dunes. And now she'd thought up a surprise for me? Likely story.

"Yes, er..." Tess fiddled with the zip of her jacket. "We had so much, um...fun. Yesterday." Her cheeks were getting even redder. "And that's why I thought we could go on a picnic now. Because, uh..."

She hesitated again, and I waited.

"You have to get to know someone, of course," she said. "Before deciding you never want to see them again, I mean. Because maybe that person's actually really nice. In real life, I mean… Right, Sam?"

She looked at me with desperate eyes and then I understood. The picnic wasn't for me. She'd changed her mind and the picnic basket was for Hugo Faber.

I had two seconds to decide whether to help her or betray her. But I didn't need those two seconds. I shrugged. "Okay."

"Come on!" both mothers cried. "It won't hurt you to show a bit of enthusiasm!"

But Tess smiled.

"Shall we hire those bikes first?" Mum asked. "Then you can go on your picnic."

I nodded. "Good idea," I said, looking straight at Tess. "On this island, it's best to have your own bike."

15

My hire bike was blue and rode a lot smoother than my bike at home. As Mum headed off to the supermarket, I turned into the doctor's car park. I was there in four seconds, and that was way too fast.

Tess had her eyes fixed on her laptop. She didn't look up until I was right in front of her. Now our mothers were gone, we didn't have to pretend any more. That was awkward, because I had no idea what to say.

Tess pushed a loose hair back behind her ear and I silently spun the top of my bicycle bell left and right. Then I rang it a couple of times, so at least something would be making some noise.

"I never say sorry," Tess said.

I looked at her with surprise. "Why not?"

"Mum thinks women say sorry way too much. She thinks women make themselves smaller than they are by saying sorry so often."

"Hmm," I said. I wouldn't have actually minded if some women were a bit smaller.

"I apologise…" Tess said. "That's the same thing. I never say that either."

I thought about it. "'I didn't mean it like that,'" I said after a while. "Do you ever say that? 'I didn't mean to leave you behind all alone' – do you say that sometimes?"

She shook her head. "That's too much like sorry."

We looked at each other. Longer than normal. Then we both started to laugh.

"That picnic…" Tess said.

"I get that it's not for me."

She nodded. "I've made a whole programme for Hugo and Elise. That's the way I planned it, so I could spend some time with them." She sighed. "Yesterday I really wanted to stop. But last night…"

I saw the hole on the beach in front of me and felt a strange tingling on the back of my neck. As if petals were being scattered over me.

"I was lying in bed and suddenly it hit me," Tess said. "This is my only chance. My father's only going to be on the island for a week. I can talk to him now. Soon he'll be gone." She looked at her phone. "I have to go. Otherwise they won't have the basket in time for lunch."

I nodded without saying anything, but inside I wanted to scream. Because this was my only chance too. I was only going to be on the island for a week. I was talking to her now. And soon I'd be gone.

Tess closed the laptop and I put my foot on the bike pedal.

"Where are you going?" she asked.

"Home," I said. "I only had one currant bun for breakfast. I'm hungry. And you don't have a picnic for me."

"Come with me then," she said. "We'll drop off the basket and then we'll get chips on the beach. My treat."

"Really?" I asked. She nodded.

I didn't get it. Why was she being nice again? Was she too scared to see her father by herself? Or was she scared I'd betray her secret? I couldn't tell. But what difference did it make? I was allowed to go with her. The story wasn't finished yet.

"Okay," I said, and Tess smiled.

16

The picnic basket was on the bright green kitchen table. Tess took seven packets wrapped in tinfoil out of the fridge and put them in the basket. I was sitting on the floor and stroking her fat tabby.

"Maybe you should give Mog a bit less to eat," I said.

"Absolutely not!" Tess said with an indignant expression. "Mog's pregnant. She's going to give birth this week. She's supposed to be fat."

"Oh," I said, looking at her fat belly with different eyes. "Who's the father?"

"We haven't got a clue."

"Really? Or are the kittens not allowed to know until they're eighteen?"

She didn't laugh. "Wait a sec," she said. "I'm almost finished. I want to show you something." She poured half a bottle of wine into an empty water bottle, screwed the lid back on and raced upstairs.

A little later she came back down with a thick, battered grey notebook. Stuck on the front cover was a postcard of a white beach with palm trees. Carefully, she put it down on the table in front of me. "Have a look."

I opened the notebook. It started with a plane ticket to Bombay. After that, the pages were covered with colourful sugar packets, ferry tickets and folders from youth hostels, all glued in. Sometimes something was written next to one of them. A date, the name of a town, or *Best temple ever!*

I leafed through from India to Nepal to Bhutan to Thailand – and then I stopped. One sentence was written under a photo of a white hotel by the sea: *Hugo could stay here forever…*

I looked at Tess. "Hugo?"

She nodded. "This is my mother's scrapbook. She kept it when she went travelling. I'm allowed to look in it because it doesn't say my father's surname anywhere. But look…" She leafed through until she came to a picture of some motorbikes. "When they wanted to rent motorbikes they had to fill in this form. The front isn't that interesting. But the glue is thirteen years old. And recently, when I was having another look at the scrapbook…"

Now I saw it too. A bit of paper had come loose.

Tess folded it back and I held my breath.

There it was, in letters that were more angular than the handwriting in the rest of the scrapbook: *Hugo Faber*.

He wasn't my father, but my heart still pounded at the sight.

"All at once I knew," Tess whispered. "I knew his name."

"So you googled him," I said, just as softly.

She nodded. "Right away. Without thinking about it. I didn't want to think about it. I just wanted to know. Who he was. If he still existed."

Quiet as a mouse, I waited for her to go on, but she didn't. "And then?" I asked.

Tess shook her head. "We have to deliver this basket first. They're counting on it for lunch."

She ran upstairs to put the scrapbook back and then we carried the picnic basket out to the bikes. It had two iron hooks that fitted over the handlebars perfectly. Tess rode in front with the basket and I raced along behind her.

It was incredible how fast the path through the dunes went when you weren't trudging along it with two sore feet. We didn't have enough breath left to talk and almost no time to get nervous.

By the time we got there my T-shirt was wet with sweat. Tess redid her ponytail at least three times and then we walked up to the house with the basket between us.

"You're not allowed to say anything," she whispered quickly, and I nodded obediently.

Hugo and Elise were sitting on the veranda reading. Hugo was wearing orange shorts and a T-shirt with a giraffe on it. I almost burst out laughing because clothes like that were too much on a dad.

But then I remembered. Hugo didn't know he was a dad.

Suddenly I felt sorry for him. It was like with dogs. If you get a puppy, you have to teach it that it's not allowed to pee inside or jump around when it's on the lead. Fathers have to learn a lot too. They're not allowed to sing in the street or make weird jokes with waitresses or wear silly clothes. But Hugo hadn't learned any of that. He wasn't a father yet. He was just a man.

"Good morning!" Tess called out. She sounded like she was acting in a toothpaste ad again. "We're here with your picnic basket."

"Lovely," said Elise. "I'm dying to know what's in it."

"Where shall I put it?" Tess asked. She was looking at Hugo, but again Elise answered.

"Plonk it down anywhere. We'll be leaving in a minute. Thanks a lot."

Hugo already had his head back in his book.

"Erm," Tess said. "The treasure hunt on the programme... Would you like to do that tomorrow or the day after?"

Elise laughed. "You know, maybe we're a little too old for a treasure hunt…"

I saw Tess's face clouding over. "Oh!" She sounded like the toothpaste hadn't worked as well as she'd expected. Like she'd just found a cavity. "Well, in that case…"

Then Hugo looked up from his book. "Of course we're not too old for a treasure hunt! I'm looking forward to it. Can we do it the day after? Then we'll have one extra day to look forward to it."

"Really?" Tess asked. "You don't think it's weird?"

"I like weird," he said with a grin.

It took her four full seconds to answer, but then she said, "Me too." Her voice was almost dancing. "I like weird too." She cleared her throat. "Okay, so we'll do the treasure hunt the day after tomorrow." She pointed at the picnic basket. "There's a plastic bottle with wine in it. And those two hooks go over your handlebars."

Hugo walked over to the basket, raised the lid and stared at the inside, which was lined with a blue checked material. "That's funny. I used to know someone with a basket exactly like this one. I haven't given that thing a second thought for years. And now I see us sitting among the buttercups again, next to a ditch lined with pollard willows. And the cherries we ate—"

I felt Tess tensing up next to me.

"That's a coincidence," I said quickly. "We've got a basket like this at home too. They're super common. Almost everyone has a basket like this!"

Hugo nodded. "Maybe..." he said slowly, still staring at the blue check.

"We're going on a picnic too," Tess blurted in a shrill voice. "I forgot to mention that." She knelt next to her father and in no time she'd pulled all the packets and boxes and bottles out of the basket. "If you ask me, this is the perfect picnic spot for you right here!" She snatched up the basket and leaped off the veranda. "Come on, Sam, we're already late for our appointment."

I had just enough time to say "have fun" before she pulled me away by one arm. Running off, I looked back for a second. The veranda was covered with sandwiches in tinfoil and forks and spoons and paper cups. And standing in the middle of all those shining packages were Hugo and Elise, gaping at us in astonishment.

17

We sped off with the empty picnic basket. Pushing down on the pedals so hard the wind whooshed past our ears. When we were a good distance from the house, Tess started screaming. No words, just "AAAAHHHHHHHHHHHHHHHHHHHHHH!"

Until she couldn't keep it up any more.

"That was horrible," she yelled. "They must think I'm crazy."

"I think so too," I shouted back. "We all do!"

She shook her head, then started to laugh. Quietly at first, then louder and louder, and in the end not making any sound at all. And I joined in. Everything in my body was fizzing and thudding and flying on breathlessly. We rolled to a stop, got off our bikes and doubled up. I'd always thought the giggles were something only girls got, but I was wrong. I had a stitch in my stomach and my cheeks were hurting and if I caught my breath for a second, I only needed to think of Hugo and Elise surrounded by tinfoil and it started all over again.

When it finally came to an end, I sighed deeply. I flopped down on the grass next to the path and looked up at Tess. "Do you really think Hugo recognised the basket?"

"One hundred per cent." She unhooked it from her bike. "I'm so dumb! I know Mum's had this thing forever. But I never stopped to think she might have used it with Hugo."

"You don't know for sure."

"I do." Suddenly she looked very serious. "That story about the delicious cherries and the ditch lined with willows – I already knew it. Mum told me exactly the same story."

"Really?"

She flipped open the lid of the basket. "Look."

In the bottom there were two small dark red hearts on the blue check.

"Blood!" I whispered.

"No, silly –" she had to laugh "– that's cherry juice." She traced the hearts with one finger. "Once I asked her how they got there and Mum told me about a picnic a long time ago. A picnic among the buttercups, on the side of a ditch lined with pollard willows. She said a very cute guy drew the hearts for her, but she didn't tell me the cute guy was my father…"

I stared at the red shapes and slowly started to understand what had happened. What if Hugo had gone on a picnic with this basket? He'd have pulled out package after package until he discovered those hearts. The hearts he himself had drawn a long time ago...

"Wow," I said. "That was quick thinking."

"Yeah. Too bad they think I'm crazy now."

I shrugged. "Better to find out sooner rather than later."

She gave me a shove. "Come on! Let's go get some chips."

18

We found a stretch of beach that was almost deserted. In the distance somebody was swimming in the sea and a man was out flying a kite by himself. It had turned cloudy and all of a sudden it was windy too, but I liked that. A sunny beach meant holidays. What we were doing was real life.

We ate our chips with satay sauce and watched the red kite do somersaults high in the sky until our boxes were empty and our fingers were grasping at thin air. Tess put her box down on the sand and looked at me.

"Do you believe everything your parents tell you?"

I thought about it. "No. Not always."

"What do you do when you don't?"

"I look it up on Wikipedia."

"Seriously?"

I nodded. "When I was six, I googled Father Christmas. It made me cry."

She laughed. Then she shook her head. "You know, I really believed what Mum said. That we were better off without my father. But one morning I started doubting it. What if she's wrong? Maybe I do want to get to know my father. Maybe I don't want to wait until I'm eighteen…"

The red kite stalled and started sagging. The man tugged on the strings and started running backwards, but it was hopeless. The kite went into a nosedive and crashed into the sand.

"While I was still trying to decide if she was right or not," Tess said, "I found his name in the scrapbook. And there was only one thing I could do. I went straight to the computer and typed in his name. I found five Hugo Fabers, but two were way too young, one had gone grey already and one had been living in Alaska for twenty years. So number five had to be my father. In twenty-five minutes I knew all about him."

I looked at her without saying anything.

"Hugo lives in Amersfoort, together with his girlfriend, Elise. That was on Facebook. He loves travelling and has an aquarium with tropical fish. He plays the trumpet in a jazz band, and I saw a photo of him ballroom dancing. The Viennese waltz is his favourite dance…"

Finally it all made sense. "And he did a woodworking course?"

She nodded.

"Wow," I said.

"Yeah." She bit her lip. "Within a day, I knew all about him, but it wasn't enough. I had no idea if he'd be a nice dad. Or if he could be bothered with a twelve-year-old daughter."

"Did you email him?"

She shook her head. "I was terrified of ruining everything. If I told Hugo Faber who I was, there'd be no going back."

There was a bit of satay sauce left in the chip box. I drew a little heart in it with one finger, then quickly rubbed it out again.

"I wanted to get to know him first," Tess said, "so I could think about whether I wanted to tell him. That seemed like the best idea. So I came up with a plan."

While her ponytail fluttered cheerfully in the wind, she stared at the grey waves with a serious look on her face. I remembered what she'd said the day before, when she asked if I wanted to dance with her: *The rest of my life depends on it.*

So this was what *that* was about. Tess didn't know yet if she was going to tell Hugo who she was. She had this week to decide: a life with a father, or a life without.

"What was your plan?" I asked softly.

The serious expression disappeared and she started laughing. "I sent an email to Hugo and Elise telling them they'd won a week in a holiday home on Texel. I wrote that our island wanted to increase tourism and that two people from each province had been selected for a free stay on Texel. Hugo and Elise were the lucky ones from the province of Utrecht."

I had to work hard to keep my jaw from dropping. "And they believed you?"

She nodded. "The only problem was making sure my mother didn't rent out our holiday home to someone else this week. A family was going to come, but I wrote telling them that unfortunately our holiday home had fallen down. And then I sent an email to my mother from a made-up email address telling her the family was sick and couldn't come." Tess looked quite proud of herself.

"Aren't you scared of your mother and Hugo bumping into each other?" I asked. "Or…" I stopped and didn't know if I should go on.

"What?" Tess asked.

I couldn't look at her. "Or is that what you want? Do you hope they'll bump into each other?"

"And fall into each other's arms sobbing? And get married next week?" She shook her head. "Hugo has

Elise. And Mum has been single for so long, she's totally used to it... She'd scream the moment she set eyes on that giraffe T-shirt. No. My mother doesn't want a husband." She stood up. "But maybe I want a father."

19

That night Jasper was back, so I didn't have the bunk bed to myself any more. He had a cast on his lower leg and he was drowsy from the painkillers. Before I could tell him about Tess, he'd fallen asleep.

I was on the top bunk and trying to keep my eyes open because I was scared of dreaming. It didn't help. I fell asleep without noticing and suddenly I could feel sand everywhere.

I was lying on my back in the shade. Tall walls rose up on all sides, like I was in a shoebox made of beach. The people were high above me. They looked down and shook their heads.

"He was only eleven," they said softly. "So many things left to experience. And now it's over."

I wanted to yell and shout that I was still alive, but I couldn't move. And then the petals started falling.

The next morning I helped Mum and Dad drag the big sofa outside. Jasper hopped out on crutches and lay down with a sigh. He had to keep his leg up all day to stop it swelling.

"What now?" he asked.

Mum, Dad and I looked at each other. It was the holidays and we were on an island. We could swim and ride bikes and fly kites and play football. But all Jasper could do was lie on a sofa. We felt sorry for him. And for ourselves too, a little.

"How about a game of cards?" Dad said.

I could tell from everyone's faces that nobody wanted to play cards, but we did it anyway.

There we were. The four of us on the patio. A family on holiday.

"We're actually really boring," I said. "A father, a mother and two children. Not very original."

"Nine of clubs," Dad said.

"I know exactly who you are," I said. "And I've known you my whole life. Or are there still some surprises?"

"Three of hearts," Mum said. And then she looked at me. "Surprises?"

"Yes! Like Dad not being our real father. Or you having three other children. Or I'm adopted because my whole family got covered by boiling lava during a volcanic eruption."

Dad nodded. "We've been meaning to tell you for a while… It was just never the right moment."

Mum and Jasper sniggered.

I scowled. "You don't get it, as usual." I didn't even know if I got it myself. But I couldn't help it. All at once I was seeing my family through Tess's eyes. What would she think of us if she happened to walk past? "If I died," I said, "would you wish you'd never had me?"

Mum shuddered. "Don't be so morbid!"

"I was wondering. Because last night—"

"Here we go again." Jasper sighed. "The professor's back in town. Everybody sleeps at night, but Sam lies in bed and thinks about things."

I looked at my big brother. "Just because you're too stupid to think—"

"Sam!" Dad snapped.

I thought right away of the day my brother got the results of his admission test. He'd thrown his desk chair down the stairs and Mum and Dad hadn't even got angry at him. They'd comforted him.

"Jasper started it," I said. "He called me a professor."

"That's not an insult," Mum said.

"Exactly!" I shouted. "Jasper doesn't even understand that professor's not an insult." Before they could all start screaming at once, I stood up. "I'm going! I'm going!"

"Stay here," Dad said. "Sam, I want—"

"Is that my punishment?" I asked. "Staying here with you?"

They stared at me. As if I wasn't their son and little brother but a strange child they'd seen for the first time that morning.

I stared back and started choking up. Because all at once I saw three people who would all be dead one day. I was the youngest, and if everything went the way it was supposed to, a day would come when I'd be all alone.

"I'm going to the beach," I said.

Nobody answered. They didn't stop me either. So I went.

20

Pedalling as fast as I could, I rode through the dunes. That night's dream was still in my head. It felt like I'd really been there, at the bottom of that beach shoebox. But that was impossible. I never dream about real things.

I parked my bike next to the wooden walkway and crossed it to the beach. It was overcast and the air smelled of grey salt. The wind made my hair stand up. The waves were thundering.

I walked straight to the hole. It was even deeper than two days ago and I couldn't understand how Jasper hadn't noticed it.

I looked around. There were dogs and joggers and kids playing football on the beach, but nobody was looking at me. I knew I was going to do something weird. It wasn't fun weird, but I still had to do it. If I did it now for real, just once, I'd never dream about it again. I never have nightmares about real things.

I climbed into the hole and lay down on the cold sand. I stretched my legs out, crossed my arms over my chest and closed my eyes.

In the hole I was sheltered from the wind, but above me I could hear the air rushing and the seagulls screeching. And through it all, in the background, never stopping, the boom of the frothing waves.

I opened my eyes.

Lying down in a hole to see what it felt like was crazy. Because when I really died, I wouldn't feel anything any more.

And suddenly I understood.

Being dead isn't so bad. You don't even notice it. Later they can scatter as many petals over me as they like. And the waves can keep on rolling. I won't miss them.

I could hear the waves now. At this moment. Because I was still alive.

I stood up and clambered back on to the beach. For a moment I felt like filling in the hole, but then a tourist would probably come rushing up and start yelling at me. Someone came here every day to make sure this hole stayed nice and deep. Someone loved this hole.

Walking back, I felt light. I listened to this moment's sea, this moment's seagulls.

But before I got back to my bike, when I was still at least fifteen steps away, I stopped. The sand had made my clothes damp and my back was cold.

Being dead yourself is something you don't notice. But when other people die, you definitely notice. You've been left behind and have to carry on. And that was the hardest thing of all. I'd seen that with Bella. And I'd seen it with Hendrik.

The light feeling vanished. Because only now did I know what I needed to do. I didn't need to practise being dead. But I could practise other people being dead. Because one day I'd have to live on without them. How would I do that? How would I cope?

I looked at my watch. It was quarter past eleven. I'd only been gone three quarters of an hour. I set the alarm to twelve o'clock and walked to the blue bench at the start of the beach. I had to practise living without Mum and Dad and Jasper for another three quarters of an hour.

I had to get used to it as fast as I could.

21

The next morning I set the alarm again as I headed off by myself. Yesterday I'd been alone for one and a half hours. Today I planned to last two.

Mum and Dad didn't like me wandering around the island by myself and wanted to know when I'd be back. But I told them exactly when to expect me: seven minutes past eleven. And then they didn't know what else to say.

I didn't feel like going to the beach, so instead I rode my bike past as many lambs as I could find. I discovered a path that cut through the fields and was so narrow you had to do your best not to wobble off it. I thought it was great until it occurred to me that this path had been specially made for people who didn't want to ride alongside each other, people who were left behind. Then I stopped smiling at the lambs.

At seven minutes past eleven I was back home, and I heard Tess's voice before I saw her. I froze.

"One more hand," she said. "And this time I want to win!"

I sneaked a look around the corner of the house. It really was her. Tess with the speckled eyes on our holiday home patio. She was sitting on the sofa next to Jasper and shuffling a pack of cards. My parents were sitting on the other side of the table. The four of them looked like a family.

"I'm not going to let you win," Jasper said cheerfully.

"And no cheating," Dad added.

"Never!" Tess laughed. She'd taken off her leather jacket because today there weren't any clouds. The wind had died down and the sun was blazing.

I looked at her light pink T-shirt and her bare arms, which were a lot browner than Jasper's. I looked at their smiling faces and felt like kicking something. Because if I was off practising for when everyone was dead, the others had no right to be carrying on their lives without me.

I strolled into view. "Hi, Tess," I said casually, walking straight past them and into the house. Now she'd met Jasper, she'd forgotten all about me. But before I'd made it through the living room, I heard light pink footsteps behind me.

"Wait!" she called.

I turned. She wasn't sitting next to my brother any more. He'd almost certainly told her about his starring role in the school musical. And he'd have definitely mentioned that he was five foot two and three quarters.

And yet here she was. Standing opposite Hatched Easter Egg Number Five.

"What were you doing?" she asked. "Nobody here had a clue."

"I went on a bike ride. But what do you care?" I swung my foot through the air. "You're having your own fun."

She tilted her head to one side and looked at me for a while. Then she shrugged. "You've lost me. But I didn't come here for your family. I came for you." She glanced quickly at the patio, but the others couldn't hear us. "I need you at the treasure hunt today," she whispered. "You have to keep Elise busy. If you two form a team, then I can talk to Hugo. Because I still haven't decided. Whether to let him be my father, I mean."

For a moment my heart had started beating faster. When she said that she hadn't come for my family but for me. But now I understood. She needed my help again. Even Hatched Easter Eggs can be useful sometimes.

"Be glad you don't have a dad," I muttered. "Saves a funeral."

"Huh?" She frowned. "What do you mean?"

"Don't you get it? Soon you'll get used to Hugo, and then he'll die!"

She started laughing. "You're nuts, Sam. I'm not going to stop getting to know people so I can save on funerals later."

"Why not?"

She stopped laughing. For a moment I thought she was going to shudder like Mum. And then tell me not to be morbid. But she didn't.

"Is that really what you want?" she asked. "To get to know as few people as possible, so not as many can die?"

I shrugged. "Maybe."

"I don't believe a word of it! And it's not something you could do anyway. You're not a lonely dinosaur. You're a human being. How many of us are there here on Earth?"

"Almost eight billion."

"See! You won't be alone even if you try. So you might as well help with the treasure hunt."

I didn't answer.

"I'm older than you," Tess said in a serious voice. "But women live years longer than men. So there's nothing to worry about. You'll die before me. Which means you won't have to come to my funeral. It'll be me going to yours."

I looked at her speckled eyes. "Really?" I asked. "Would you do that?"

She nodded.

22

I think I was even more nervous than Tess when the treasure hunt started. She'd been used to weird her whole life, but I was just a beginner. What did Hugo and Elise think of us? They'd won a week in a holiday home and now they had to go on a treasure hunt with two children. That really was weird.

Tess had sneaked out that morning to prepare the route, so we could start right away. With a map full of crosses, the four of us walked into the dunes.

We were a man, a woman and two children, but that didn't mean we looked like a family. Hugo was wearing trainers with flashing lights and a yellow T-shirt with DO NOT FEED written on it in big letters. Elise had made a garland of beach grass and was wearing it like a crown. If I was a police officer with an important question, I would definitely ask Tess or me.

Trailing along behind the others, I thought again about Tess saying she'd come to my funeral. It was crazy, but it made me smile.

In a dry, sunny dip in the dunes, we found our first task. Tess spotted the hidden CD player almost immediately, but that was no surprise. She'd put it there herself. "There's a letter!" she cried excitedly. She unfolded it. "Listen to these five songs. The first person to say the singer's name gets three points per song."

The warm ground was covered with rabbit droppings and prickly branches, but we didn't care. The four of us sat in a circle around the CD player. The air smelled of hay and sea breeze, and I felt like we were on a school camp. A perfect, carefree school camp.

Tess pressed PLAY and we held our breath.

First there was a rustling sound. Then vague piano.

The moment a trumpet started to play, Hugo slapped his knee. "Louis Armstrong!" he yelled.

Tess started beaming, until she realised she had to act like she didn't know if he was right or not. Quickly she opened the envelope with *1* on it and then nodded seriously. "Well answered, Hugo Faber. Three points for Team A." With the next song, she screamed the answer herself after the very first word. "Ella Fitzgerald!" She opened the second envelope and, you guessed it – she was right. Hugo gave her a high five and she was beaming again.

"Come on," I said, a bit annoyed. "I've never even heard of these people!"

I knew the treasure hunt wasn't meant for me. But I still had to get used to the idea of being completely crushed.

"Don't you know Ella?" Hugo asked in surprise. "She was a fantastic jazz singer." He looked at Tess. "You were really fast."

"Ah," Tess said modestly. "Sometimes you get lucky."

The other numbers were all jazz songs too, of course, and Team A scored all fifteen points.

"Time to find the next treasure!" Tess cried cheerfully, and we set off in search of the next cross on the map.

It was by far the most unfair treasure hunt I'd ever done. Elise and I didn't score a single point, while Team A soon had more than fifty. The questions were about aquarium fish and ballroom dancing or countries Hugo had been to on holiday. Tess put on a frown, acted like she was thinking hard, then gave the perfect answer.

I hate losing, but gradually I started to enjoy myself. Because Tess looked happy, I felt happy too, on the inside. When father and daughter were standing quietly side by side, only their speckled eyes were similar. But now they were winning a treasure hunt together, there were lots of things that showed they were related. When they got a question right, they both stuck their chin in the air in the same way. They were as fanatical as each other when they had to fish tinfoil zebrafish out of a bucket. And when they were walking in front of me, I saw that they put their feet down the same way too. With their toes turned out a little. It was a happy walk. And cute too. At least when Tess did it.

At the end of the treasure hunt we came to a deserted lake tucked away in the dunes. The water was as smooth as glass and reflected the blue sky. On a sandy part of the shore we found two big pieces of wood with tools next to them. Of course, I thought. There was still one of Hugo's hobbies we hadn't covered yet. Woodwork. I shook my head. It was incredible. How had Tess managed all this? She must have spent weeks preparing everything.

She picked up the envelope, which was on the sand, weighed down with a hammer. "*For the last task you have thirty minutes,*" she read. "*Make an animal from this piece of wood. If the man at Sea View Beach Restaurant can tell which animal it is, you get twenty-five points.*"

"You're always so lucky!" Elise laughed, giving Hugo a shove. "You did that course last year. I don't even know how to hold a chisel—"

"The clock starts now!" Tess screamed.

Elise and I trotted over to our piece of wood.

"Which animal shall we make?" Elise whispered.

I looked doubtfully at our lump of wood. "A hippo?"

She giggled. "Good plan."

I grabbed the saw while Elise studied an unknown tool from all sides. The beach-grass garland on her head was crooked, but she was still as cheerful as at the start of the treasure hunt. She didn't care that we were losing. Sometimes I saw her looking over and smiling at Tess and Hugo, who were hard at work on their block of wood. Then I realised I was doing the same thing. I was happy to watch Tess and her father without bothering too much about our hippo.

"Will you take the rasp?" I heard Tess say. "For its back."

"Okay," Hugo said. "Then you can make the fur with a gouge."

I kept watching them. And then I thought of my own dad. I'd known him my whole life, but we had never gouged and rasped hippos together. Why not? Why didn't we have a single hobby in common?

"Ow!" Hugo shouted. Then he groaned and my blood turned cold, like that first day, with the hole on the beach.

"Hugo!" Elise gasped. She dropped her tools and started running.

"What is it?" I cried, running too.

97

But Hugo didn't need to answer. We could see what it was.

There was a gash at least two inches long in his hand, under the thumb. Gaping raw flesh with blood pouring out of it. More blood than I'd ever seen coming out of a person before. It was running down his wrist and dripping on the sand.

And standing next to Hugo was Tess. She was holding a sharp metal thing that could only be a gouge. Her face was white and she wasn't moving, just staring at the wound.

"Oh!" Elise said in a faint voice. "I can't bear the sight of blood." She covered her eyes with her hands and sat down.

Hugo swore and I saw Tess flinch. "I'm sorry," she whispered. "I really am incredibly sorry. I—"

"Don't worry about it," Hugo said, but it didn't sound like he meant it. He looked at his bleeding hand. "This needs stitching, that's obvious."

"There's not a hospital on all of Texel," I said. "You have to take the ferry to Den Helder."

"Not true," Tess said quickly. "You can get things stitched at the doctor's. I—" She stopped mid-sentence.

I looked at her. And then I understood. We had to go to the doctor's. And who worked for the doctor? Who was the first person you saw when you walked into that low, grey building? Exactly. Tess's mother. We stared at each other.

"No…" she whispered. She shook her head. "That can't happen."

"What?" Elise asked from the ground. "What's going on?"

"It needs stitching," I said, looking urgently at Tess. "We don't have any choice."

There was nothing to be done: today Tess's mother and father were going to see each other for the first time in thirteen years. Tess's mother would be sitting at her desk and would see Hugo as soon as he walked in through the door bleeding.

They'd recognise each other, of course, because grown-ups don't change much in thirteen years. It said DO NOT FEED on Hugo's T-shirt and he had fairy lights in his shoes, but Tess's mother would still know who he was.

They would talk to each other and then Tess wouldn't be able to stay a secret any longer. Hugo would hear that he had a daughter, whether Tess wanted him to or not. From then on, she wouldn't be free to choose if she wanted to have a father.

She had a father. And she'd just gouged a hole in him.

23

Tess and Elise were no use.

"They mustn't see each other," Tess whispered, her hands shaking. "That whole plan... I wish I'd never come up with it. I should have listened to Mum..."

"All that blood!" Elise groaned. "My knees have turned to jelly."

I looked around. There were no police in sight. No lifeguards and no lighthouse keeper. We had to do it all ourselves. Because if we didn't do anything, Hugo's funeral might arrive a lot sooner than expected.

"Everyone quiet!" I shouted. "This isn't helping. Tess, what's the quickest way back to the house? We have to get to the car as fast as we can." I took off my white T-shirt and gave it to Hugo. "Here, wrap this around your hand." I looked up at him. "Can you walk?"

"Sure," he said. "No problem." He was pale, but not nearly as pale as his girlfriend or his daughter.

Elise slowly got up and the four of us set off. The sun was warm on my bare shoulders and for a moment it felt like an exciting finale to our treasure hunt. But then I looked back at Tess's face. For her, this wasn't a one-day adventure. It wasn't a cut that needed stitching and would heal. She'd wanted to choose for herself whether to tell her father. And now she couldn't.

Silently we followed the narrow rabbit track. We were walking fast, but not running. Blood was soaking through my white T-shirt, but Hugo didn't say anything. Elise was keeping her eyes fixed on the ground. Tess sighed deeply. And I was searching for a solution.

Come on, brain! I yelled inside my head. You're always thinking, right? You give me nightmares and make Jasper call me a professor. Make yourself useful for once!

And then suddenly I knew what to do.

"Tess!" I shouted. Nice and loud, because it didn't matter if Hugo and Elise heard me. "Give me your phone! Here in the dunes you don't have any signal, but in the holiday home you do, right?"

She nodded.

"Okay, listen. I'll run ahead with your phone, and then I can call the doctor's to tell the receptionist we're coming. We had to do that with Jasper's ankle too."

She looked at me and I could tell from her expression that she didn't understand. How could calling her mother help?

"Give me your phone!" I demanded again. And then, under my breath, "It'll work out, I promise."

She still didn't understand, but she gave me the phone.

"She's under MUM WORK," she whispered. "This path will take you straight there."

I ran as fast as I could and made it to the house in five minutes. Panting, I searched through her phone and called the number under MUM WORK – EMERGENCY ONLY.

"Is this Tess's mother?" I shouted when she answered. "It's Sam!"

"Sam?" a stern voice asked. "Sam who?"

I sighed. "The tiny tourist!"

"Oh, why didn't you say so? What's up, tiny tourist?"

"There's something wrong with Tess. You have to come home right away."

"But why?" her mother asked calmly. "Put Tess on. She knows I'm at work."

I'd thought my plan out up to this point and now I didn't know what to do any more. I needed to lure Tess's mother away so she wouldn't be there when Hugo arrived at the doctor's. But how could I convince her? My own mother would have raced home the moment she heard there was something wrong. I was sure of that. But Tess's mother was not so easily worried.

"Sam?" she asked sternly. "Why won't you put Tess on? Is this a joke?"

"No, really it's not! Tess can't come to the phone because she's…um…crying. She's crying so much she can't talk."

"I don't believe it. Tess never cries."

I looked around. In the distance I heard the others approaching. I was running out of time. Tess's mother had raised a whole kid all by herself. She didn't scare easy.

And then I knew. "Tess is pregnant!" I shouted down the phone. "She just found out. She won't talk to me. She's locked herself in the bathroom and—"

"I'm on my way." Her mother hung up.

I heard the phone beeping and stood there for a moment.

What had I done?

24

Tess and I threw our bikes into the boot of the blue Saab, while Hugo headed for the driver's seat.

"Hugo," Elise yelped. "You can't drive!" She led him round to the other side of the car and sat herself down in the driver's seat. Her hands were shaking and I could tell she was still dizzy.

Very slowly, she set the Saab in motion. Then she accidentally looked to the side and saw the blood-soaked T-shirt wrapped around Hugo's hand. She closed her eyes for a moment as she steered the car around a bend.

On the back seat, Tess and I hardly dared breathe. Tess with a gouge – that was scary. But an upset Elise at the wheel of a car – that was terrifying.

I couldn't say anything, of course, so I quickly typed out a message for Tess on her phone. She read it on the screen:

HURRY HOME. I TOLD YOUR MUM YOUR PET GNAT, SO SHES GONE HOME. KEEP HER THERE TILL HU GOES GONE!

Tess raised her eyebrows. "My pet gnat?" she asked softly.

I shook my head impatiently and grabbed back the phone. PREGNANT, I typed. YOU'RE PREGNANT!

She read it. "But that's not even possible!" Her voice came out as a high squeak, and the Saab swerved.

"What?" Elise asked nervously. "What's going on?"

"Nothing," I said. "Nothing's going on."

Tess glared at me. "How am I going to explain that?" she whispered.

I shook my head because I didn't have a clue. She bit her lip. Her cheeks were blazing.

The moment the Saab stopped in front of the doctor's office, Tess threw open the door. She jerked open the boot and pulled out her bike. Mine fell clattering to the ground, but Tess already had her feet on her pedals. "I have to feed Mog," she called out to Hugo. "I forgot to do it this morning. I'm terribly awfully sorry about the cut. Really!" And then she raced off.

I didn't find the Mog excuse particularly believable, but Hugo and Elise didn't seem to be listening and hurried into the grey building. I came in behind them. I was still without a T-shirt, but I couldn't help that.

This time I didn't pay any attention to the smell of plasters. The coughing in the waiting room didn't matter. Only one thing counted: who was sitting at the desk.

I stretched my neck and bent to the side, but I couldn't see anything because Hugo and Elise were bunched together in front of me. It wasn't until they stopped that I could see the receptionist.

It was a lady I'd never seen before.

I leaned on the cold wall because all of a sudden I felt a little dizzy too.

"Come with me," she said. "I'll let the doctor know you're here right away."

They disappeared into a small white room and I took a deep breath.

I'd done it.

Hugo and Tess's mother hadn't met each other.

Tess could still decide for herself whether to tell Hugo Faber who she was. She could still choose. A life with a father – or a life without. And if she told him, she could do it her own way. Without blood. Without a yelling doctor's receptionist.

It was just a shame her mother now thought she was pregnant. For a moment I considered going to their house. But that didn't actually seem like such a good idea. It was too dangerous with all those cactuses.

I walked back outside, picked up my bike off the paving stones and rode out of the village. I'd lived more than long enough today without a father and a mother.

25

I thought at least four dozen times about calling Tess, but I didn't. I was too scared. And she had my father's number. So she could call me when she wasn't pregnant any more.

The next morning, I had to do some shopping with Dad because Mum had another migraine. Dad wouldn't have minded going by himself, but Jasper and I didn't think that was such a good idea. If you let my father loose in new supermarkets, he always buys strange things.

We drove to the village while Mum stayed in bed. When she lay completely still on her back without seeing a glimmer of light and not hearing a sound, the headaches weren't as bad. That meant keeping the blinds down and earplugs in her ears.

My poor mother. If there was anybody who was used to things being stupid, it was her. How did she do it? She was always cheerful even though she knew a migraine could start at any moment.

"I'm not scared of them," I heard her tell a friend of hers once. "When there's pain, there's pain. It can't be helped. And when I'm not in pain, I'm happy. Because there's no pain." It sounded simple. But I was sure it was complicated.

In the supermarket Dad steered the shopping trolley while I ran around grabbing barbecue sausages and part-baked bread rolls and strawberry yoghurt. And then, in the confectionery aisle, I almost ran straight into Tess.

"Hey!" I cried out in surprise.

Her basket was packed with chocolate. I saw Twixes and cherry liqueurs and Guylian seashells and chocolate raisins.

"How did it go yesterday?" I asked. And I leaned closer to whisper, "Are you still pregnant?"

She giggled. "It was terrible." Tess tried to put on a serious expression, but only half succeeded. "I couldn't say it was all fake cos Mum would have gone straight back to work. And then she'd have seen Hugo after all. So I had to drag it out forever and act like I really didn't know a thing about getting pregnant."

"Ha ha…" I said, as if I knew everything about getting pregnant.

"So I told Mum that something had happened at school behind the bike shed with Dennis. And that now I thought… Because Dennis… Well, I don't know… How can I explain it?"

"You don't have to drag it out for me," I said. "What happened with Dennis?"

She giggled again. "Exactly… That's what my mother wanted to know too. After three quarters of an hour I told her. Dennis held my hand behind the bike shed at school. And that's why I thought I was pregnant."

I frowned. "But why did this Dennis kid hold your hand?"

"He didn't, silly! I made it up. You don't think I'd actually hold hands with someone behind the bike shed?"

"Oh," I said.

She sighed and grabbed a bag of Chokotoffs. "I didn't like having to fool my mother like that. But I'm glad she didn't see Hugo."

"Because you want to tell him yourself who you are?"

She nodded.

"Are you going to?" I asked. "Are you going to let him know he's your father?"

"I think so. During the treasure hunt—"

"He was great on the treasure hunt!"

"Yes." Her whole face seemed to glow. But then she looked at her full shopping basket and the glow disappeared. "Maybe he won't want me," she said anxiously. "I gouged a really deep hole in him. Who'd want a daughter who's that clumsy?"

"Of course he wants you! Who wouldn't want a daughter who's such a good gouger?"

She sighed again. "I'm going to buy one of every kind of chocolate. With the last of my pocket money. And then I'll take him a whole boxful."

"What are you going to say?"

"What do you think? That I'm very, very sorry, of course."

"Is that right?" I asked. "I thought you never said sorry. I thought you said women already say sorry way too much."

It didn't make her laugh.

"You know," she said. "I've avoided a lot of sorries so far. Mum too, her whole life. I think I'm entitled to say it once now."

She put another seven chocolate bars and a selection of handmade chocolate truffles in her basket, then headed for the checkout. I grabbed a bag of M&M's and went looking for Dad.

26

After we'd packed all the shopping into the car, Dad stood there for a moment. "I actually wouldn't mind getting a haircut…"

"Feel free," I said. "I'll entertain myself."

I wasn't even surprised because Dad always wants to get a haircut when we're on holiday. It's his special treat. Other people buy souvenirs; he gets new hair. Generally it makes his head look weird and square, but that's part of the fun. If he wanted to look normal, he'd go to the hairdresser's at home.

I watched him wandering off and thought, what if I hadn't already known him eleven years? What if I was seeing him for the first time today and he told me he loved getting holiday haircuts. Because of the adventure. What a funny, interesting man, I'd probably think. It was bad luck for Dad I'd already known him so long.

After he'd disappeared round the corner, I hurried over to Tess's house. Her gigantic mother was at work and Tess had gone to visit Hugo, so no one would mind me picking some daisies in their front garden.

A little later I rang the fairy-tale grandfather's front door with a tiny bunch of flowers in one hand. It took a long time for the door to open and I was starting to get worried. But finally I heard some shuffling.

"Young man!" Hendrik was standing bent over in the doorway. He was still wearing the clothes from four days ago, but that seemed fine to me. There was only one tiny little stain on his shirt.

I held up the daisies. "For Remus."

He didn't look surprised. He led the way into the garden and I lay the daisies down under the apple tree, which had lost almost all its blossom. Together we looked at the freshly turned earth.

"Slice of cake?" Hendrik asked after a while, and I nodded.

We sat outside on a wobbly bench that was pushed up against the house. Hendrik drank a cup of tea while I ate the cake, which had gone a little stale but still tasted good.

"It's quiet without Remus…" the old man said.

I sighed. "I can imagine. That's why I've started practising."

"Practising?"

"Yes. I need to get used to how stupid it is."

Hendrik shook his head. "I don't follow."

And then, while the last apple blossoms fell, I started to tell him. I told him about Bella's father and the hole on the beach. And that I'd started practising being alone. A little bit longer each day. So I'd be used to it later.

When I was finished, Hendrik stood up silently to go and get me another piece of cake. It took a long time.

"I'm eighty-nine years old," he said after he came back, "and that's the daftest thing I've ever heard." He sat down again, making the bench creak. Then he turned and studied me carefully. His eyes were greyish blue. The colour of the North Sea. "I lost my wife more than seven years ago," he said. "For seven years I've been sitting on this bench by myself. What do you reckon? Do you think I wish I'd seen Maria less while she was still alive? Do I wish I'd gone off cycling on my own, and talked to her less?" He stared hard at me. "Would that make things better now?"

The cake lay untouched on my plate.

"When my Maria died," Hendrik said, "I cried because I hadn't seen her enough. I wanted more Maria. Not less."

I turned towards the apple tree to avoid looking at his face.

"I wish I knew why green was her favourite colour," Hendrik said softly. "Which books she read when she was little…"

He had to stop talking. I didn't even know what Mum did every day at work. Or if Dad could dance. Or why Jasper had been acting mean towards me for weeks now.

"And what she dreamed about. I wish I'd asked her lots more questions. I wish—"

"Stop it!" I blurted. "I get it. You miss her. You've made your point."

Hendrik was quiet for a moment. "How old are you?" he asked after a while.

"Eleven and six weeks."

"Well, with any luck, nobody will die in your life for a long time yet."

"That's what they said to Bella. And then her father died."

"No one can know for sure." He put down his mug. "But this I do know. Getting used to being alone won't do you any good at all. Do you think your friend Bella wishes she'd seen her father less while he was still alive? Would that make it easier for her now?"

I shook my head. Of course she didn't. Bella would be crazy to wish for something like that.

"See," Hendrik said. "You're the daftest little boy in eighty-nine years."

And I knew he was right.

"I have to go find my dad," I said, getting up off the bench.

Hendrik nodded. "Of course."

27

That night I slept like a log. No nightmares. And when I woke up, it was already half past nine. I couldn't believe I'd wasted that much time.

Still wearing my pyjamas, I gathered up all the games I could find and at 9.37 exactly I emerged from the holiday home with the whole pile. I dropped them on the garden table and looked at my family, who were all reading.

"Game time!"

They looked up in surprise. The Texel hairdresser really had turned Dad's head into a square, and you could tell from Mum's face that she'd had a migraine yesterday. She always looked a bit crumpled afterwards.

"Jasper gets to choose," I said. "What are we going to play first?"

My brother lowered his comic. I could see him hesitating. And then he sighed. "You always think Risk takes too—"

"We're on holiday," I said. "We've got all day." I pretended not to notice his astonishment and grabbed the box.

They'd have to get used to it, me being there. I was the youngest, after all. They were going to have to talk to me and play games with me for the rest of their lives. They were better off getting some practice.

When Tess showed up a couple of hours later to ask if I wanted to go to the beach with her, my family seemed a bit relieved. At first I was annoyed, but then it occurred to me that they'd only just started practising. It was okay if they took their time to get used to me again.

On the way to the beach Tess couldn't stop talking. Hugo hadn't been angry with her at all. He thought the box of chocolates was fantastic and he'd asked if we wanted to go kite-flying with him today. Because the treasure hunt had ended on such a downer.

"That's so nice of him!" She was out of breath but she went on anyway. "He's only known us for a couple of days and he still asks if we want to go kite-flying!"

I didn't need to say anything. It was enough just riding my bike and looking at her glowing face.

When we parked our bikes at the beach, she grabbed me by the arm. "I'm going to tell him today," she said. "Who I am. Who he is."

"Really?"

"Yes. I've made up my mind."

We were standing still, but it was like we were dancing.

"I'll tell him after we've finished flying the kite. Maybe you could make sure Elise is, um…"

I nodded. "I'll keep her busy while you go for a walk on the beach with your father."

She bit her lip. It was a mystery to me how she could breathe at all.

"What will he say?" I asked. "When you explain… How do you think he'll feel? Suddenly finding out he's got a daughter! That he's been a father for twelve years without…"

She shook her head in silence and then we heard Hugo calling in the distance. He waved to us. He had a white bandage on his hand but otherwise looked perfectly healthy.

"I'm terrible at flying kites," he said when we got closer. "So I'm in dire need of your assistance!"

It was perfect. Elise had brought lemonade and cold pancakes, and for a change Hugo was wearing a plain blue T-shirt and jeans without any holes in them. He almost looked like a dad. Tess dared to mention other things occasionally besides jazz and aquarium fish, and she was the best kite-flyer on the whole beach. I was sure Hugo liked her.

Everything was perfect. Until it fell apart.

It happened while we were sitting down to have a break. We were munching pancakes sprinkled with sugar and a little bit of sand and watching the seagulls strolling along the wet part of the beach. Far out at sea the sailing boats were shiny white triangles and the sky was criss-crossed with jet trails.

I let the fine sand and tiny pieces of shell glide through my fingers and looked at the people around

me. I'd never seen the beach this busy. The adults were calmly sunbathing, but the children wouldn't stay still for a second.

There were too many to count. The little kids were wearing sun hats and hitting each other with plastic spades. The bigger ones were throwing balls and Frisbees and inflatable dolphins at each other and almost drowning when they tried to jump over the waves. The beach was swarming with children and they were yelling and screeching and laughing and howling so much you could hardly hear the sea. It was like all the animals had escaped from the zoo at once.

And then it happened.

"Pfff!" said Hugo. He looked at Elise. "I'm so glad we don't have kids." He smiled at her and she smiled back.

"I was thinking the same thing," she said cheerfully.

The waves pounded. The children screeched. But all of a sudden everything seemed deathly quiet.

I didn't dare look at Tess. I felt a hole in my stomach and knew that the hole she felt must be much, much bigger. And that it hurt.

She stood up. It took quite a while before she was able to say anything. "The pancakes were delicious," she managed at last, but the voice didn't sound like hers. "Unfortunately I have to go home now. I forgot to feed Mog."

I stood up too. My body felt heavy, and that was funny. It should have felt lighter now there was a hole in it.

"The lemonade was delicious too," I said. "I always help feed Mog. So I have to go now too."

Together we walked back to our bikes. Tess didn't give her father another glance.

28

Tess never cries. That's what her mother said. But she was crying now.

She didn't want to talk to me. She wanted to go home. I was scared she wouldn't be able to see where she was going because of the tears, but she'd been riding her bike along these paths her whole life and I could barely keep up with her.

We rode until just before the village and then she stopped. She didn't want to ride past all the shops crying. "Go home," she said, rubbing her cheeks with both hands.

"No," I said.

Next to the bike path was a huge tulip field, flowers planted next to each other in dead-straight lines. First a thick band of red, then purple, then canary yellow, then pink. As far as you could see.

"Hugo didn't mean it like that—"

"He did mean it like that!" Tess shouted. "Didn't you see the look he gave Elise? He smiled at her. He was relieved. All the other people on the beach had been dumb enough to have kids. But he'd escaped."

The coloured stripes billowed in the wind. I'd never seen a tulip field this close before. Close to the road you could see every flower separately. In the distance you only saw colour.

"No, seriously," I insisted. "He didn't mean to be cruel. He didn't know his daughter was sitting right there next to him."

"Exactly! He didn't know, and that's why he was able to be honest."

I looked at her face and saw the hole. It was everywhere. There was a little bit missing from her cheeks. From her arms. And from her eyes.

"He's your father," I said. "You get on really well. And you're like each other because he likes weird too. You want him!"

"But he doesn't want me." She pulled an elastic out of her pocket and bundled her hair into a tight ponytail. "Remember when I left you behind in the dunes?" she said. "I was angry because you said it was simple. But now it really *is* simple. Hugo doesn't want kids. He's happy with his life the way it is. He's got a girlfriend. And he's got lights in his shoes. I'm not going to tell him he has to be a father."

"But he *is* a father!"

She shook her head. "As long as he doesn't know, he's not a father. Tomorrow he's going back on the ferry. He'll probably never come to Texel again. It's over."

"But—"

"This was always the plan, remember? I was going to see if I wanted to tell him who I was. And now I know." She wiped her nose one last time with the back of her hand, then got back on her bike.

I went to say something, but she beat me to it.

"Stop, Sam! Stay out of it. In a couple of days you'll be gone too. Then we'll never see each other again. What difference does it make to you if I have a father or not? This is my life and I'll decide what to do with it."

I wanted to shout that she'd promised to come to my funeral. She'd promised to know me for the rest of my life. But that promise obviously didn't matter any more. Hugo didn't want her. And now she didn't want me.

She rode past the red stripe and the purple one, the yellow one and the pink one.

She got smaller and smaller. And then she was gone.

29

"Jasper," I whispered from the top bunk after we'd gone to bed that night. "Are you asleep yet?"

"Yes," he mumbled. And then, a little more awake, "What?"

"You have to help me."

"Yeah, sure," he said. I could tell from the bed that he'd turned over.

"Really," I said.

"What can I do for you? Blow your exams? Break a leg? Or ruin your life? I'm good at all three of those."

In the light his voice only sounded angry. But now, in the dark, I heard something else in it. I didn't know what it was.

"What do you mean?" I whispered. "What are you good at? Ruining my life? Or yours?"

"My own, of course," he snapped. "But I'd be happy to ruin yours too if you like."

I almost threw my pillow at him. But then I thought about it. I sat up. "What are you on about? You've got a lead role in the musical. You're almost five foot three. And you get on better with Dad than I do. What's ruined about your life?"

He mumbled something.

"What?" I asked.

"I'm thick!"

"Of course you're not. Idiot."

"You say so every day."

"That's just to tease you… Like you calling me a professor. That doesn't make me one either."

"But I am," he said. "I'm too thick to go to the school I wanted to go to. And everybody knows you're crazy clever. All the teachers say so. When you grow up you can be anything you like. Except maybe a pilot. You're too short for that."

"I'm gonna grow!"

"But I'm never going to get any smarter," Jasper said.

His words hung in the air, filling the dark room. And I couldn't think of anything to chase them away.

"I'd swap places with you," I said quietly.

Yesterday, when Tess still wanted to come to my funeral, I wouldn't have said that. But that was then.

Of course Jasper wasn't thick. Maybe – if even the teachers said so – he wasn't quite as smart as me. But you don't need that extra cleverness. Thinking usually only gets you into trouble.

"Ha!" Jasper sniggered. "I am so not gonna swap with you. Then I'd be teensy. And I'd have to think about dinosaurs drinking tea with hedgehogs. No way!"

And then I really did throw my pillow at him.

30

The pillow fight with Jasper made me forget I wanted to ask him something. And that was why I had to work it out all by myself that night.

Tess said it was her life and I had to stay out of it. And now I was wondering if that was true. Did people really have to stay out of other people's lives? Or could you stay out of them too much?

I thought about Tess and her mother, who decided everything on their own.

Whether to stop travelling or not.

Whether to have a baby.

Who was going to win the treasure hunt.

Whether or not to have a father.

And all that time, Hugo Faber hadn't had a say in anything. His own daughter was walking around on the planet and he didn't have the faintest idea. He'd been allowed to see Tess with the speckled eyes for just under a week. And now it was over. Was that fair?

When it grew light again, I knew I was going to do something terrible.

It was worse than practising being dead. It was worse than making up a pregnancy for Tess. Because this was about a real pregnancy. A secret one from thirteen years ago.

During breakfast I looked at Mum and Dad and Jasper. I couldn't tell them anything because I knew what they would say. I mustn't do it. It wasn't my business.

But I was still going to stick my nose into it.

"I'm sorry," I said, "but I have to go for another bike ride. Tomorrow we can play Risk all day. I promise."

This was the longest ride of the whole week. I wasn't riding through the dunes but on a path right on the coast. The view was fantastic. Along the sea there was a tall dyke and the bike path was halfway up that dyke, on the same side as the water. On the black velvety asphalt, it felt like I was flying.

The sea glittered and shone. Racing along, I smelled seaweed and rotten fish and sunshine. Sometimes it looked like the path ended in the waves, but when I got there it curved round a bend and a brand-new ribbon of dark asphalt stretched out before me.

I kept my head empty because I didn't want to think. If I started thinking, I'd stop pedalling and turn back. I'd realise I was about to do something that wasn't allowed at all.

But this just happened to be my life. And like Tess, I decided for myself what to do with it. I was eleven and I wasn't afraid of anything any more. I understood now what Mum meant when she talked about her headaches. Because it was the same with death. When it was here, it was here. And when it wasn't, you should be happy.

When I saw the port in the distance, my heart started pounding. There was a long line of cars waiting for the next ferry. One left every half hour. From Den Helder to Texel. And from Texel to Den Helder. When Jasper broke his ankle, he'd got stuck in the traffic jam with Dad too.

In the hospital they'd told Jasper that sometimes an ambulance went on the ferry. It came from Den Helder to pick up someone on the island and the ferry didn't leave until the ambulance had come back again. All so the sick person wouldn't have to wait in a traffic jam.

The bike path along the coast ended, so I had to take a detour to get to the port. Out of breath, I rode past the waiting cars, searching for a bright blue Saab. But the car wasn't there yet. Or it was already gone.

I couldn't go back now. I didn't want to go back. Instead I waited at the end of the line and checked every car that came to join the queue.

No blue Saab.

No blue Saab.

No blue Saab.

And then, after three quarters of an hour, when I'd already given up and could hardly even remember what I was doing there…

A blue Saab.

And not just any blue Saab. The number plate was right. It was Hugo and Elise.

"Sam!" Hugo called when he saw me. His hand wasn't bleeding any more, so he was allowed to drive again. "What are you doing here?" he asked through the open side window. "You haven't come here for us?"

"I have," I said, and then I couldn't get another word out.

I'd only known him for a few days. And I'd only known Tess a few hours longer. It wasn't my business. I had to stay out of it.

And at the same time I thought, I know something ginormous about this man. I can't let him drive off without telling him who he is. I looked into his speckled eyes and suddenly I knew. This wasn't about him. He was nice, but I could get along fine without him. This was about Tess.

I knew she'd never forgive me. But I was still going to do it.

31

In the distance, the white ferry was approaching the port. Seagulls were flocking around it and there were people standing at the railing. A car behind us beeped.

"I have…" I cleared my throat. The sun was burning the back of my neck. The ferry kept getting closer.

"Would you…" I stopped again. "Could you take the next ferry? There's something I have to tell you." I looked at Elise. "Something I have to tell Hugo."

He frowned. "You have to tell me something?"

"Yes. A secret."

Elise laughed. "A real secret? That's exciting!"

But I kept my eyes on Hugo. He had to see that it wasn't a joke. In a few minutes his life would be changed forever. Maybe he didn't want Tess at all. Maybe he didn't want any children. Even now, when he already had one. But he had to decide that for himself.

"It's not my secret," I said. "But I'm going to tell it anyway."

Hugo was quiet for a second, then nodded. "Okay. We'll take the next ferry."

"Really?" Elise asked in surprise.

I wheeled my bike out of the way so Hugo could pull out of the queue. He parked the Saab next to a picnic table and bent over towards Elise for a moment. Then he got out of the car.

Yesterday, on the beach, I hadn't understood how Tess could still breathe. And now I felt like my lungs had seized up. All that time, I'd thought Tess would tell him. She'd tell Hugo who she was. I'd tried to imagine that conversation between father and daughter but hadn't been able to.

How do you tell someone he's been a father for the last twelve years? Do you do it slowly and carefully? Or in one rip, like taking off a plaster?

"Here," said Hugo, sitting down on the picnic table with his feet on the bench. He was wearing pink flip-flops. And a black T-shirt with bones on it: a white spine, ribs, collarbones. Like you were looking through him with an X-ray machine.

I was way too nervous to sit still, so I just stood there.

"I'm listening," he said.

I twisted the heel of my shoe into the sandy ground. "Nobody knows I'm telling you this," I said. "So if I've told you and you don't want it, then we'll act like it never happened. Then it will stay our secret."

"That sounds serious," Hugo said. "Is it about you?"

I shook my head. "It's about you. And it will change your life. But maybe you don't want that at all. Maybe you're happy with Elise and lights in your shoes and you don't want anything else. And if you are, then you can act like you've never heard what I'm going to tell you."

"Sam…" He ran his fingers through his hair. "You're starting to make me a bit nervous. Can't you just tell me what's going on?"

I nodded. "Tess is your daughter."

For three seconds he was quiet. Then he started laughing. "Don't be daft, she can't be! I don't have a daughter." He shook his head. "What makes you think she's my daughter?"

I didn't say anything.

"Do you think we look like each other? Is that what gave you the idea?"

I stayed quiet.

"Or was it because the four of us had so much fun doing that treasure hunt?" He wiped his forehead and pulled a packet of chewing gum out of his pocket. "Want one?"

I shook my head. Then I crossed my arms and stared at him. "Thirteen years ago, you went travelling around the world with your girlfriend."

"How do you know that?"

"You flew to Bombay and travelled from India to Nepal to Bhutan to Thailand. After a few months your girlfriend broke up with you and went back home."

Hugo had gone deathly silent. He forgot to chew his gum and listened.

"When she got back to the Netherlands, she found out…" I stopped. "I don't know her name. I only know her as Tess's mother. What was your girlfriend's name when you went travelling around the world?"

"Ida," he said. He shook his head. "This is impossible…"

"Back in the Netherlands," I said, "Ida found out she was pregnant. She didn't tell you and had the baby on her own. So you became a father without knowing. Tess is twelve now. And she's your daughter."

He was paler than if he'd just been gouged again. "I don't believe it," he said hoarsely. He squinted at the shining sea. Then looked straight up at the sky. "Ida would have told me."

"She didn't tell your daughter anything either," I said. "Tess only just found out what your name was. By accident, in her mother's scrapbook. Do you remember that scrapbook? A thick grey notebook that Ida kept during your trip?"

He nodded silently.

"Once Tess knew your name, she googled you. And then she made up a plan to lure you to Texel. Because she wanted to get to know you. She wanted to find out if you were nice or not before deciding if you were allowed to be her father."

"But… Why didn't she say anything? Didn't she like me? Didn't she want me?"

I sat next to him and watched the ferry sailing back out of the port. New people were standing at the railing. The screeching seagulls were following it again.

"She thought you were amazing. Yesterday, on the beach, she wanted to tell you who she was. She'd decided. But then you said how happy you were not to have any kids. And that changed everything."

He covered his face with his hands and shook his head. Then he wiped his forehead again. He looked less like a grown-up than ever. More or less the same age as me. But with pink flip-flops. And a skeleton on his T-shirt.

"I meant what I said before. You can pretend you haven't heard anything. If Tess told you, there'd be no going back. But now I'm telling you and I don't have anything to do with any of it. I'll never see her again. If you don't want a daughter, you don't have to have one. You just take the next ferry to Den Helder."

"But I have a daughter!"

"Exactly. That's what I keep telling Tess."

He stood up. "I have to see her. I have to talk to her."

"Really?" I asked excitedly. "You want to see her?"

He was still pale. "Of course I want to see her."

32

I stayed behind at the picnic table while Hugo went back to Elise. I squeezed my hands together and waited.

After eleven minutes he stuck his head out of the side window. "You coming?"

"Can I?" I asked.

"Course. It's all your fault, after all."

I jumped off the table. "Are you going to her house?"

He shook his head. "We'll try the holiday home first. That's where she was when we left. She said something about cleaning, so I hope she's still there."

He put my bike on top of their bags in the boot and I sat on the back seat. Elise looked super serious. I'd never seen her like that before. She was biting a bit of skin next to her nail and her eyes were fixed on the floor.

"I'm sorry…" I told her while the Saab turned back the way it had come. "I know you're glad you don't have any kids. But Tess is already twelve, so she doesn't spend the whole day screaming. And she's toilet-trained. Maybe it won't be too bad."

Elise didn't say anything.

"And she won't come to live with you, of course. She lives here on the island. With her mother. But maybe she can come to visit sometimes. In the holidays, for instance. Or when—"

"Sam!" Hugo shouted. "Stop. Put a sock in it for a few minutes. Please. Let us get used to it, okay?"

The car raced past enormous fields of flowers. I looked at the brightly coloured stripes flashing past and counted how many different colours there were. I got up to seven.

Hugo and Elise were silent too, trying to get used to it. To Hugo's daughter, who would now be a part of their lives forever. After eleven years my parents still weren't fully used to me, so I knew things like that can take a long time.

And then Elise turned towards me. "Was Tess very sad?" she asked. "When Hugh said he didn't want children?"

I nodded. "She cried. And that's something she never does otherwise."

"The poor thing…" Elise said.

I looked at her face with surprise. Because I could see she was already a little bit used to it. Maybe she didn't even know it herself yet. But she was adjusting.

We drove on, and I found it really hard to keep my mouth shut. There were so many things I wanted to tell them about. About the treasure hunt. About the cherry blood in the picnic basket. And about Tess, of course. But I'd said enough. The rest was for her.

The closer we came to the holiday home, the more nervous I got. Hugo now knew he had a daughter. But Tess still didn't know I'd betrayed her secret.

The flat fields changed to dunes. The grass got coarser and less green. A fluffy rabbit shot across the road and a little later we were driving through pine forest with patches of sunlight. And then we'd reached the holiday home's drive.

Hugo's hands squeezed the steering wheel hard as he drove the last little bit. Elise rubbed his leg but didn't say anything.

Inside the Saab we were used to the throb of the engine, but I knew you could clearly hear the car approaching from inside the house.

Hugo stopped the car and turned off the engine, and for four seconds we waited in silence.

Then Tess appeared on the veranda. I saw her look at the Saab, but I didn't have a proper view of her face.

Elise and I stayed where we were, sitting completely still.

After seven more seconds Hugo finally came back to life. He undid his seat belt, opened the car door and climbed out.

And then he just stood there.

"Go on," I whispered, though I knew he couldn't hear me. "Go over to her!"

But he didn't dare.

With Hugo not moving, Tess started walking towards the car. I could see she was surprised, but she must have thought Hugo and Elise had forgotten something.

That was when she saw me sitting in the car.

Tess froze.

She looked at Hugo and then back at me. And then slowly shook her head. As if this was a complete disaster. As if it was the last thing in the world she wanted.

33

I got out of the car. I had no choice.

Tess walked up to me and stopped in front of me. "What have you done?" she whispered.

I looked at Hugo, who was still rooted to the spot. The bones on his T-shirt were shining in the sun.

"I couldn't let him go," I said softly. "Not without telling him."

"Have you lost your mind? I didn't want him to know. I told you that! How could you..." She shook her head and I saw tears in her eyes. "Really? You told him?"

I nodded. "Just now, when he was waiting for the ferry."

I saw her swallow. Her father knew who she was. And now she had to face him.

It took a while before she found the courage. "Hugo... I didn't want..." She took a step towards him, then froze again. "Sam's mad! He had no right to tell you. I know you don't want any children. Please just forget about me."

Hugo slowly shook his head. "I'm sorry. But that's not the plan."

"What?"

"I'm not planning on forgetting you."

"Why not? That'll work!"

He looked at her with a serious expression on his face. "I don't want any screeching kids swinging spades around. But I do want you." He hesitated. "I mean…I have you. You exist. I've got a twelve-year-old daughter. And now I know, I want to get to know that daughter of mine better."

"Really?"

He nodded. He took the last steps forward and wrapped his arms around her. Tess wrapped her arms around him too. And they didn't let each other go.

I could see they still weren't used to it. Half of Tess came from Hugo, but they'd never touched each other. He'd never thrown her up in the air when she was little. He'd never held her hand crossing the road.

But for a first attempt, this was a fantastic hug.

They'd just have to practise a bit more.

34

They let go of each other when a phone started ring-ing. Tess grabbed her mobile, glanced at the screen and turned red. "My mother…" She looked at Hugo. "Sorry, I just…"

He nodded. While Tess answered the phone, Hugo walked over to Elise and gave her a big hug. You could tell they practised every day.

"Hey, Mum!" Tess quickly turned her back on us. "Really?" I heard her ask. "Oh, wow! How many so far…? Yeah, I'm in the dunes with Sam, but I'll come straight home. Tell Mog to wait with the rest. See you soon!" She turned back towards us. "Mog's giving birth! Mum found her in the attic. She'd gone up there to hide and she's already had two kittens. I—" She stopped. She looked at her father and I saw her face change. "No, that's ridiculous. I'll see the kittens later. I'll stay here, of course. Would you like something to drink? Tea, or lemonade, or…" She started walking towards the house, but Hugo didn't budge.

"No way," he said. "We're going to go see Mog."

Tess stopped. "Really?" she asked. "You want to come with me to see Mog?"

He nodded. "I don't want to miss a single birth from now on. And I have to talk to your mother. There's a few things we need to discuss…"

Tess stared at him. The whole holiday she'd been thinking about whether she wanted Hugo Faber as her father. But now he knew the situation, he wanted things himself. Now Hugo Faber was deciding what was going to happen. And that took some adjusting.

"Um…" Tess said. "Can you maybe wait a bit with that discussing?" Her voice sounded higher than usual. "Until I've prepared Mum?" She shot an uncertain glance at her father. "My mother is fantastic. And she looks after me really well. But if she hears what I've done, I'm going to be grounded for the rest of my life."

"We'll see about that." Suddenly Hugo didn't look like a little boy any more. "Ida's going to have to explain why I've got a twelve-year-old daughter I didn't know anything about. Maybe she's the one who's going to be grounded."

Elise let out a giggle. But she quickly changed back to serious.

"Tess's mother is really tall," I said. "Most men are scared of her."

"Not me," Hugo said, as if the idea had never entered his head. "Anyway! She's on her own. And there are four of us. We can stand up to her."

35

Once more, Tess and I were sitting together on the back seat of the Saab. Tess was a nervous wreck, but she still found time to squeeze my arm.

"Ow!" I whispered.

"That's nothing compared to what I wanted to do to you just now," she said sternly. "I still can't believe you told him. He'd almost left the island…"

"I'm sorry," I said.

"I'm not." She squeezed even harder. "He wants me!"

I looked into her eyes and saw that the hole had disappeared.

Much too soon, the Saab stopped in front of the house with the daisies. It took a full minute before anyone said anything.

"Hmm…" Hugo already sounded a little less sure of himself. "How exactly are we going to do this?"

"I'll go in first," Tess said. "To make sure she doesn't have a heart attack."

I cast a worried glance at Hugo. "They've got five cactuses on the windowsill. And all the colours are really bright."

"Shall I just stay in the car for the duration?" Elise asked. "I don't think I—"

Just then somebody knocked on the window next to Tess. Ida's giant head appeared and a shock passed through the car. Tess's mother looked into the car. First at her daughter. Then at me. And then she saw Hugo. Her eyes grew large. She'd recognised him immediately.

"New plan!" Hugo exclaimed. "Everyone out of the car."

And that's what we did. We stood opposite each other on the pavement, Tess's mother on one side and the four of us on the other.

"Mum…" Tess said, but she didn't know how to go on from there.

"Maybe I should…" Elise stopped.

And then Tess's mother shook her head. "Hugo," she said in a severe voice. "That is the most hideous T-shirt I've ever seen."

Tess gaped at her mother. "Mum! You don't say things like that."

"I do," said Ida.

And then Hugo started chuckling. "You do." He shook his head. "You haven't changed a bit."

148

It was as if the situation was only just starting to get through to Ida. She looked from her daughter to Hugo, then back at her daughter. "How—"

"I found his name," Tess said. "In the scrapbook."

"That's impossible!"

"I still found it." Tess crossed her arms. "And then I invited Hugo to the island to get to know him. All week he had no idea who I was, but now he knows. He doesn't actually want children. But he wants me." She stood very tall and stared directly at her mother. Only now did I see how alike the two of them were. Tess had Hugo's speckled eyes and his enthusiasm. But the rest had come straight from her mother.

"Come inside," said Ida. "We don't need to put on a show for the whole street." She walked to the front door and Tess and Hugo followed her. I hesitated, and so did Elise.

"Should we leave them alone for a while?" Elise whispered.

"Probably," I said. "Yes."

We looked at each other.

"Was that long enough?" she asked, and I nodded. We hurried inside.

In the living room everyone stood around awkwardly. The cactuses on the windowsill were flowering.

"I can't believe it," Ida told Tess. "This is about our life together! I thought you were fine not having a father. No man sticking his nose into everything. Why didn't you tell me? How could you keep it secret?"

Tess was about to say something, but Hugo laid a hand on her shoulder.

"Ida," he said calmly. "Don't act like you tell everyone everything." He shook his head. "We have a daughter together! You were pregnant. And you didn't think it necessary to even let me know?"

She looked at him and for the first time that week I saw hesitation in her face. It made her look gentler. She was about to say something, stopped herself, bit her lip and then began talking after all.

"Remember I phoned you when you were in Vietnam? A month after I'd come back to the Netherlands?"

He nodded.

"I wanted to tell you then," she said. "That I was pregnant. But all you could talk about was the Swedish girls you'd met there. How fantastic they were. And that you were travelling on together. And so I didn't tell you."

"Really?" he asked. "Was that it?" He shook his head. "I was making stuff up…I only hung out with those girls for one evening. But I was angry because you'd walked out on me. I was just saying things. I had no idea it was going to cost me a daughter."

They looked at each other for a while in silence.

Then Hugo put his other hand on Tess's other shoulder. "She's found me now. And I'd love to get to know her. If that's allowed."

"Yes," Ida said, and in that instant she didn't look scary at all. "Of course it's allowed."

36

Elise left to go for a walk. She said she wanted to explore the village, but it was clear she was trying to give Hugo some time alone with Ida and Tess. And then I couldn't stay any longer either, of course.

"Bye, Tess!" I said loudly.

No answer.

"Will I see you tomorrow?"

She didn't even look at me. She was way too busy with her father and her mother. And with the kittens. She still had to go and see them too.

I got my bike out of the car and rode off by myself. The sun was shining and the sea breeze was blowing and the little lambs were frolicking, but all at once I felt indescribably sad. Because suddenly it was all over. Hugo and Elise would go home this evening. And we – I hadn't even thought about it yet – were leaving tomorrow. We didn't have any time left for Risk. No more time for swimming or barbecuing or flying kites.

And no more time for Tess. We were going home. And she was staying here on the island.

Riding along a narrow dyke between two fields, I understood what she had meant at that tulip field. What did it matter to me whether she had a father or not? What did I care? I wouldn't even notice the difference.

Of course, I was glad for her. More than glad. I was happy for her. After twelve years she finally knew who her father was. She could get to know him. She could go and stay at his house. And now she knew where her speckled eyes came from.

But for myself I was sad because I saw a list in front of me of the most important people in my life. The people I'd save if a volcano erupted. Or rescue from a shark. Mum and Dad and Jasper came first, of course. But number four on that list wasn't someone from my class at school. Not someone from football, or from our street, or one of my cousins.

Number four was Tess. I'd only known her a week. But if there was one person I wanted to come to my funeral, it was her.

I threw my bike down on the ground next to our holiday home and walked around to the patio. Jasper still had to keep his leg up, so he was lying on the sofa like always. Dad was stringing beans and Mum had the laptop on her knee. "Sam!" she called out when she saw me. "We were getting worried."

I flopped down on to a chair. "Really?"

"What do you think?" Dad asked. "You left in the morning and the afternoon's half gone already. If Tess hadn't told me on the first day about Texel not being dangerous—"

"And you've been disappearing for hours on end all week." Mum shook her head. "That's got to stop. We let you because we've had such bad luck with Jasper's ankle. But from now on you have to stay with us. Don't go more than ten yards away."

They were both trying to look very strict. That's something they're not good at, and I hope they never learn. They're cute when they try to set rules.

"Fine," I said. "Staying with you is exactly what I want to do."

"Yeah, sure," said Jasper. Then he kept his gaze fixed on me. "What have you been doing all day anyway?"

It was a real question. Not one you can answer with a shrug. And he hadn't looked straight back at his comic. He was waiting for an answer.

I sighed. "I was helping Tess get a father. Her own father, I mean – not just anyone. She didn't know him. And now she does. That's what we were doing all week."

"Really?" Jasper asked.

Dad didn't grab any more beans. Mum shut her laptop.

"It kept us super busy," I said. "First we had to bury a canary and then arrange a picnic basket and do a treasure hunt. But during the treasure hunt Tess's father got wounded… And just when Tess had decided to let him be her father, it all went wrong. But it all turned out well in the end. For her, at least."

They stared at me.

"I couldn't tell you before," I said. "Because it was top secret. Besides Tess, I was the only person in the whole world who knew about it."

Dad shook his head slowly.

"And now?" Jasper asked. "Isn't it secret any more?"

"No, everyone's allowed to know now."

"Great," he said. "Then tell us all about it. But start at the beginning, because so far it doesn't make any sense at all. And that's not because I'm dumb. It's because you're nuts."

"Jasper…" Mum said, but I started laughing.

"Really?" I asked. "Do you want to hear the whole story?"

They nodded.

37

"Heavens," said Dad, when I'd finished telling them.

"Oh, Sam," Mum said. "I can hardly believe you told Hugo he has a daughter. Thank goodness it turned out well."

"Man!" Jasper cried. "You've had the best holiday ever."

I sighed. "But now it's all over. Hugo and Elise will be leaving soon and tomorrow we'll take the ferry too. I'll never see Tess again."

"Can't you go round tonight?" Mum asked. "Just for a very short visit."

I shrugged. "They're busy with the kittens. And Tess will want to spend all her time talking to her dad. Not to me."

"Do you really not want to say goodbye?" Dad asked. "I'll drive you."

"I'm coming too!" Jasper shouted. "We know Tess too, don't we? And we saw her giant mother when I broke my ankle. Now I want to know who her father is too."

"I told you…" I shook my head. "They're busy with the kittens. They were born today."

"No problem," Jasper said. "Then we've got something to celebrate. A birthday party! We'll take balloons and streamers. Come on, I've had the most boring week of my life. I want to see that T-shirt of Hugo's too!"

My parents laughed, but I kept thinking about those balloons. When Jasper was born, Mum and Dad had decorated the living room. I'd seen the photos. Proudly they held their baby in their arms and all around them were brightly coloured balloons they'd hung up. And there was a similar set of photos from when I was born.

I sat up straight. I knew what we had to do. "We don't need balloons for the kittens," I said, "but for Hugo! He missed out on everything when Tess was born. But today he got a daughter. We have to celebrate that."

My parents looked at each other.

"We could just drop by?" Mum said.

"I think it's a lovely idea." Dad jumped up. But then he stopped. "Oh! The shops are all shut…"

He sat down again and I sighed. Without balloons, our visit didn't make any sense. We'd just be going there to stick our noses into things that weren't our business. All Tess wanted was to be alone with Hugo. She'd made that clear.

"I know!" All of a sudden Jasper started laughing. "Remember we saw a house in the village where they were having a birthday party? They had balloons up everywhere. I'm sure they'll lend us some."

I looked at him with my mouth hanging open.

"What?" he asked.

"That's the most brilliant idea I've ever heard."

He nodded contentedly. "I thought so too."

"Come on!" said Dad. "Let's go before Hugo and Elise disappear on the ferry."

38

In the car we almost died laughing. The birthday party was over, so the people at the house had given us dozens of balloons and we'd crammed so many into the back of the car that there was hardly any room left for Jasper and me. Mum was in the front passenger seat trying to keep them from blocking Dad's view of the road.

"Slow down a bit!" she cried. "These balloons are going everywhere."

"Ha!" he said. "If you were a bit faster they wouldn't get past you!"

"Turn right here!" I called out. "And then the second left."

Now we were almost there, I was starting to lose my nerve. What would Tess think of me turning up on her doorstep with my entire family? Still, I didn't tell Dad to turn back. I wanted to see her. One last time before we left. That was the minimum for someone who was number four on my list.

Dad helped Jasper with his crutches, and then there we were in front of the door. For a second I remembered that I was the youngest. And that I would be left by myself. But then I thought, forget it. I don't have time for things like that. We're alive and standing on a garden path. The daisies are in full bloom right now. And soon, in a few seconds, I'll see Tess again. I'm better off worrying about that.

So that's what I did. Mum rang the doorbell and my heart pounded like it was trying to escape.

After eleven long seconds Tess's mother opened the door. She looked from me to the bunch of balloons and then at my family.

"Tess!" she yelled. "The tiny tourist's here again. And this time he's brought his family."

Without saying anything else, she stood there waiting for her daughter. After fifteen seconds Tess came bounding down the stairs with Hugo close behind.

"Sam!" she cried. "I wanted—"

But I didn't let her finish. "These are for you." I held up the balloons. "Or for Hugo really. Because he never got to celebrate when you were born."

There they stood, the three of them. Hugo, Ida and Tess. Father, mother and daughter. They weren't a family. But they were family.

Hugo looked at the balloons silently. He may have been wearing a cool T-shirt with bones on it, but his eyes were glistening. Elise came up next to him and took his hand.

"Of course, the balloons are partly to celebrate the kittens," I told Tess. "But mainly because of you."

"To celebrate me?" she asked.

I nodded and felt my cheeks turn red.

"I'll second that," said Hugo. "Three cheers for Tess!"

Ida sighed and beckoned everyone in with both hands. "Come in, everyone, come in. There's no point trying to resist the tiny tourist, I've learned that by now. After going to all this trouble, you may as well have something to drink. Have you met Hugo yet?"

39

We'd hung up almost all the balloons. There was one yellow one left.

"We need that," Tess said, grabbing the balloon and pulling on my arm with her other hand. "Come on, Sam."

I saw our mothers giggling.

"She's a bit bossy," Ida whispered to Mum. "She gets that from me."

They were sitting next to each other on the sofa and drinking white wine. Dad and Jasper were all ears listening to Hugo, who had some great stories to tell. Elise was sitting next to him, smiling.

"Where are we going?" I asked, as we walked down the street with the balloon.

"Hendrik's," Tess said. "I had an idea. He says he's too old for a new pet, but that's rubbish. He might live in that house for years yet. All alone. So he's going to get one of our kittens on loan. And when he can't look after it any more, the kitten will come back to live with us."

I stopped walking.

I couldn't do it any more. She was chattering so cheerfully. Her blonde hair was glowing in the evening sun. Her speckled eyes were shining. She was number four on my list. And this was the last time I'd ever see her.

"What's wrong?" she asked.

I shook my head.

"Tell me!"

I swallowed. And then I shrugged. "It's just…I never like saying goodbye. That's what's so stupid about dying. Never seeing each other again. I hate that. I still do."

She frowned. "But I'm not dying." She held up the balloon. "I've just been born!"

"What good is that to me?" I said in an angry voice. "If I never see you again—"

"What?" she asked. "I don't get it. Who says you'll never see me again?"

"You! Yesterday at the tulip field. You asked what difference it makes to me if you have a father or not. We're never going to see each other again anyway."

She started to laugh.

"That's not funny!" I shouted.

"You ninny," she said. "Of course we're going to see each other again! I'm coming to your funeral, aren't I?

Or had you already forgotten that? We're going to be seeing each other for the rest of our lives. And in the summer holidays we're going to stay with Hugo and Elise. Both of us."

"What?"

"Get used to it," she said, smiling. "I decide everything. I'm not only in charge of my own life, but yours too." She tugged on the string of the balloon so it bounced off my head. "In the summer I'm going to stay at Hugo and Elise's, and they want you there too. I think that makes me a bit less scary. Hugo's already promised to make a treasure hunt for us, and you can be on Elise's team again. She likes you. And then I'll be on a team with Hugo."

"But if he's made the treasure hunt, you'll win again!"

"Of course." She laughed and started walking again. "Come on, we're going to see Hendrik. And then back to our parents. To celebrate us!" She started to swing the yellow balloon in circles over our heads. "For we're two jolly good fellows, for we're two jolly good fellows…"

I looked around. There was nobody out on the street. But so what if there was? We loved weird.

So we sang the rest together. As loud as we could.